THE SECOND RISING SUN

LOUISE G. SIMONE

authorHOUSE®

AuthorHouse™
1663 Liberty Drive
Bloomington, IN 47403
www.authorhouse.com
Phone: 1 (800) 839-8640

Published by AuthorHouse 01/28/2017

ISBN: 978-1-5246-6919-5 (sc)
ISBN: 978-1-5246-6917-1 (hc)
ISBN: 978-1-5246-6918-8 (e)

Library of Congress Control Number: 2017901338

Print information available on the last page.

This book is printed on acid-free paper.

CHAPTER 1

CHRISTINE STORMED INTO SAM'S office. Taken by surprise, he blurted out, "What's wrong?"

She answered hysterically, "Nancy has gone!"

Sam, bewildered, asked, "Christine, what are you talking about? Gone where?"

Christine screamed, "She's gone! She left Japan! She went back to the United States with David Watson. I found this note in her room. They're going to be married as soon as possible."

Sam became distraught. "Why, Christine? Why would she just up and leave?"

"Why?" She threw the note at him. "Here—read it for yourself. There's no more happiness here. We haven't been a family for a long time. She doesn't want to be a part of your insanity any longer. She's going back with David to make a better life for herself."

She paused for emphasis. "I came here to make a better life for us, Sam. But you hung me out to dry. If it wasn't for Nancy and my work at the labs, I would have gone insane a long time ago.

"For years you haven't given me or her the slightest indication that you were even aware of our existence. Sam, your thirst for revenge has become an addiction far overshadowing all the success you have achieved throughout the years. People will only remember you as the fanatical supergenius who destroyed the world."

Her description fueled her anger and frustration as she became more intense. "Sam, you have accomplished a herculean feat. You have climbed the highest mountain, and your consortium is one of the most powerful in the entire world. Now you're trying to shove your success up the whole world's ass!"

Sam retorted, "Well, Christine, isn't that what it's all about? Isn't that what we always wanted to accomplish?"

"No, Sam, not we. It's your obsession. The blinding hatred left my body many years ago. It disappeared when I first came to Japan and started working with all those young women. They had only one unselfish thought in mind. They just wanted to bring a normal, healthy child into this world."

Sam just listened as Christine continued. "There's nothing wrong with this world. What's wrong is the concept that some people like you can't forgive and forget. You have spent your whole life building a powerful empire. The sole purpose was to satisfy your pent-up hatred. You will get your revenge while you destroy an entire country, the country of your birth. Youth—"

Sam managed to cut in momentarily, yelling back at her, "My family and I tried for over twenty-five years to be Americans—good Americans—but they wouldn't let us. They never accepted us, and I always believed that they never would."

Christine's anger had gone beyond the boiling point. All the years of frustration, of just standing by and watching him wield his mighty ax, had suddenly surfaced in one mighty eruption. She wouldn't give him any slack until she got it all out. "Maybe you think you were the only one who was hurt. Well, I've got news for you! We were all hurt, but time has healed our wounds and we have gone on with our lives. Except for you, Sam. Your hatred has grown so large that you need a giant conglomerate to carry it around in."

Without taking a breath, she continued with her tirade. "Eventually your hate will wrap itself around the whole world and squeeze it so tight that it will explode in your face. Maybe you are the one the gods have chosen to push the button that will end the world."

Christine had to leave before she said something she could never take back. Feeling the extreme weight of her frustration and mental fatigue, she slowly turned and walked over to the door. She grasped and turned the ornate handle of his immense office door and left.

Sam clutched the arms of his chair so tightly that his hands turned blue. He remained frozen in his seat, her words echoing through his mind. He felt as though he had been whirling in the funnel of a tornado. It was fortunate that the storm left without blowing him out of the window.

His wife still had a lot of spunk even though her rage had been suppressed for many years. Christine left Sam with a lot to think about as he sat there alone reflecting on the past. He realized that a lot of what she said was true. He was still too numb to realize it was all true. Despite her furious but righteous verbal assault, the old boy wasn't quite ready to capitulate. All she had succeeded in doing was getting his adrenaline flowing again.

CHAPTER 2

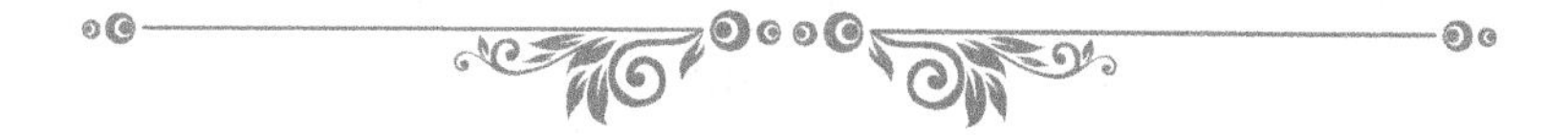

SAM'S PARENTS, KEI AND Fumiko Sagarra, left Japan for America during the Roaring Twenties. They landed in Chicago, immigrants with a definite but unique purpose. Most immigrants came to make a better life and to find their fortune in the legendary streets paved with gold. However, Sam's parents already had a good life and plenty of assets.

Sam's grandfather headed the Japanese coalition of heavy equipment manufacturers. He was its leader almost from its conception. The coalition, under Grandfather's guidance, had chosen Sam's father to go to America and open a new frontier for their products.

At this time the Japanese conglomerate was manufacturing trucks, buses, farm equipment, and small two-passenger automobiles. The consortium even had a shipbuilding facility that produced cargo ships, which they sold to foreign countries. The largest market that eluded them was the American market. It seemed that every time they were close to making a deal, it would slip through their fingers. Invisible barriers had existed between the two countries for many years. These barriers had to be overcome, and Sam's father was chosen for the job. He definitely had his work cut out for him.

Japanese credibility had always been in question. The American importers never believed the Japanese could produce or deliver what they promised. They were concerned about making big commitments with Japanese companies. The Americans felt that the companies were heavily influenced by their government. At that particular time, Japan had a democratic government. The Americans believed a short circuit was inevitable, and it would send the Japanese economy into a tailspin. Everything would come tumbling down, including their commitments and the big bucks they'd have invested. Kei Sagarra's task was enormous. He had to convince the American giant that *Jack could deliver!*

Kei rented a house in a prestigious upper-class area of town. Even though they were in a different country, the Sagarras carried with them their beliefs about class separation. They wouldn't even consider living in the Japanese quarter, which was in the poorer section of the city.

What the Sagarras were not prepared for was that they would not easily be accepted in the part of town they had chosen. They eventually purchased the house they rented, but it would take more than ten years before they were recognized and referred to as neighbors. This came about only by a miracle of fate.

After settling in, Father rented a small office in the heart of town. It was convenient and strategically located. He could use public transportation to reach the manufacturers, whose corporate offices were nearby. This would also show Grandfather and the consortium that although he had chosen an expensive neighborhood in which to live, he was still a frugal man when it came to business.

Conducting business would not be easy. Father was different from the normal crowd of salesmen making the rounds of the manufacturers.

He would call for an appointment and introduce himself in perfect English; he had mastered the language in college. In later years, he told his children funny stories about the facial expressions of some of the people he had made appointments with over the phone. When Mr. Kei Sagarra arrived for his designated appointment, they expected to meet the usual hotshot salesman. All of the buyers were amazed when a dignified Japanese gentleman walked in. He definitely stood out.

Being a born optimist, Father believed this was an advantage he had over the other salesmen. He said that everyone else looked alike and became a jumble in the manufacturers' minds. The easiest thing to do was to give the order to the Jap, which they did.

Unfortunately, most of the orders he received were only for minor products and accessories. The main purpose of his coming to America was to expand the Japanese consortium's market to include heavy equipment and automotive products. It seemed that the United States already was saturated with these products. The American heavy-equipment manufacturers seemed to be fulfilling the country's needs.

The Japanese cars with their small engines were not what the consumer wanted. American cars were bigger, and the engines were more powerful. The manufacturers kept trying to outperform each other by building even larger cars with still more powerful engines.

The Japanese cars were compact, with much smaller engines. The technology for more powerful engines and the need for them hadn't reached Japan yet. As history would show, it never did. Japanese manufacturers would stick to the compact car and eventually develop technology to pack more power into the smaller engine.

The years that followed were mixed with frustration and confusion for Sam's father. Every time he thought he had made some progress, the American mob bosses were all over him. He was not above dealing with them. In Japan and other foreign countries, it was a natural part of doing business. In America if you weren't of the proper ethnic descent, the road ahead was bumpy and usually led to dead ends. Even the Jews were able to notch out a small piece for themselves, but a Jap—*no way!* An intelligent Japanese businessman was too novel an idea for the American conglomerates to consider.

CHAPTER 3

Sam came roaring into town six weeks prematurely, on January 21, 1922, at 10:45 p.m. Mother would use this as a means of cutting him down to size. When he did something to disgrace or anger her, she would remind him of the inconvenience he had caused her on that extremely cold January evening. It was snowing heavily when suddenly she had to leave her warm comfortable home, unprepared, and rush to the hospital to give birth. She said, "Sam, it was totally inconsiderate of you to do that to me." His mother always kidded him about it, but she couldn't help smiling as she said it.

Brother Charlie blew in fourteen months later in March. Mother had a similar story to relate to him. She told him how strong the wind was blowing and how heavy the rain was coming down.

It wasn't easy raising children in Chicago in those days because of all the violence around them, especially when some of the kids pretended they were certain mobsters. This occurred often because the gangsters had attained their own peculiar brand of hero status. It was quite natural for the children to emulate their heroes because they didn't fully understand what the mobsters were doing wrong. The newspapers gave front-page coverage to the often bizarre killings and chases that crossed state lines. Children avidly read all the accounts and translated them into their own game of cops and robbers. In their games, someone always got killed and sometimes it was a good guy. The good guys were not always the cops.

Somehow Mother managed to keep them under control in those turbulent times. Father was definitely the head of the house, but the strength and backbone of the family emanated with Mother. Every time the children did something wrong, their biggest fear was "How are we going to explain this to Mother?"

Mother and Father Sagarra gave their children American names, thinking it would make them more acceptable. Sam remembered asking his mother, when he was about twelve, why she had named him Sam instead of using a Japanese derivative. None of his cousins from Japan had names like Sam or Charlie. She explained that it would make their assimilation into American society much easier.

Sam didn't understand what assimilation meant, and he asked her, "Is it something like pasteurization?"

She said, "Assimilation is not like pasteurization. Assimilation is the process of blending in foreigners that come to a new country and getting all the different races and religions to work together in harmony."

Reflecting back now, Sam was not so sure that she was right. He thought that pasteurization was a better term. He remembered how many times he was brought to the boiling point throughout his teenage years. His family was never really accepted. Their names certainly were American, but they looked different and Mother couldn't change that. They were the ones who had to accept that fact and learn to live with it.

Sam always felt that even though he was of Japanese descent, he was first and foremost an American. As children, he and his brothers and sister were accepted by their peers. As they entered their teenage years, however, that racial difference was pushed down their throats continuously. It had a lot to do with the times. America's relationship with Japan was becoming strained, and it affected the way people thought of them. What the future had in store for them would challenge their belief that they were American citizens beyond anyone's imagination.

Times were becoming more difficult for Sam's father as well, as he wrestled with the giant octopus of an obligation that his family had chosen for him. Mother became pregnant once more and presented her husband with twins, a girl and a boy. The little girl was named Sarah, and the chubby little boy, who seemed to be about twice the size of Sarah, was named William, who was always called Billy.

At special family get-togethers, in times to come, the children would jokingly praise their father for what a truly remarkable man he really was. "Surely," they would say, "you must have been superhuman to be able to untangle yourself from that octopus and spend some time with Mother so she could be given the honor of bringing us into the world."

CHAPTER 4

THAT'S HOW LIFE BEGAN for the Sagarra children. They were four American kids with Japanese parents. Growing up in Chicago, they were as American as apple pie. They loved American food, especially hot dogs, and their language was filled with slang and colloquialisms. They all loved football and baseball and played these sports as well.

Except for Sam, none of his brothers or his sister could speak any Japanese at all. Father, being the first born and naturally the oldest, thought Sam should be taught the Japanese language and traditions. Sam was required to attend a class two days a week, on Sunday mornings and Monday after school. The class was given by a small group of Japanese "Issei," or first generation in America. Father and other Japanese businessmen organized and sponsored this school to teach young Japanese children. The children born as American citizens were called "Nisei," or second generation. The main purpose of the school was to teach and try to keep alive the language, customs, and traditions that were part of their Japanese heritage.

The Sagarra children all attended the same local public schools. Sam was the first to start and paved the way for the rest. He was the only Japanese student in the school. Mother referred to Sam as the "pathfinder," but he never really understood what that meant. He certainly stood out, and the kids looked at him cautiously at first and were very careful not to get too close. This was the first grade, and up until now nobody had ever seen anyone like Sam. Curiously, within a few days, he had become friendly with most of the class and was asked to join in all the activities. The other children even went as far as holding his hand when they had to.

Maybe that's what Mother meant when she referred to him as the pathfinder; however, "shock absorber" would have been a better term. When the other brothers and Sam's sister started school, hardly anyone noticed their presence. Why should they? After all, the school already had one Japanese student, and as the saying goes, "They all look alike."

Elementary school became a basic routine. The children participated in all the sports. Sam's brothers loved baseball and got to be really good at it. Sarah excelled in swimming. She was short but had strong legs. She could stop, change directions, and take off again as though she was shot out of a cannon.

By the time Charlie and Sam got to high school, they had already gained a reputation for being tough competitors. Charlie was only a freshman, but the baseball team was waiting for him. The coach watched him play in junior high because they badly needed a catcher. Charlie had a strong arm. Not only was he a great catcher but he also could throw a ball to second base with such velocity that most players didn't try to steal. He was only five feet six inches at the time, but he tipped the scale at 199 pounds. Charlie was a great catcher, and he literally covered home plate.

Charlie became very popular with the girls and was also a good student scholastically. He was always upbeat. Despite his weight, he was light on his feet and always greeted someone with a big smile that sort of made his eyes twinkle. The kids loved him and so did Sam.

Sam excelled at football, and in his senior year, the team picked him to be captain. His teammates developed a special bond. Most of them had been playing together since their freshman year and could almost read each other's thoughts. When the team finished junior year, it was number one in the city division. In its final year, the team took an oath to be number one in the state.

The football coach told the team that he had been watching the professional teams at practice. He wanted them to develop some of the plays that were being used. Sam was chosen to play on offense. Coach wanted someone fast with big hands, and Sam fit the bill. He was made a wide receiver.

One of the plays required him to take off as the ball was snapped, run twenty yards down the field and turn and catch the ball that had already been thrown. The secret to the play was timing. After having the ball bounce off the back of his head a dozen or so times, his brain had had it! He could almost hear it saying, "Sam, if you're going to keep this up, just put me on the bench. Let them continue throwing the ball at your fat head without me in it."

Four days later they were back on the field, still feeling the effects of the last practice session. The coach gave Sam some new pointers. He said, "Sam you're turning too late." Sam had kind of figured that out for himself. So on this day, he tried running a little faster and turning sooner. It was fortunate for Sam that he had his mouth closed or the football would have been the first of its kind to have a full set of its own front teeth. Eventually, they got into sync. The whole team got their act together, and they were more than ready for the new season.

CHAPTER 5

SAM'S MOTHER ALWAYS INSISTED that all the children had to come home for dinner. If one of them was late, she would make everyone wait. She firmly believed that dinnertime was a time for the family to share thoughts with one another. If someone had a problem, they would all try to help solve it. Most importantly, Mother believed that family sharing would create a bond that would last forever.

Most of the time the children looked like a bunch of battle casualties. Sam had his lips stitched because of a collision with a football, and Charlie didn't look much better. He had spike marks on his legs and bumps on the side of his head from wild pitches. Sarah was sore, scratched, and bruised from her swimming practices. She had the strength and speed needed for the sport, but she was still learning how to control the accuracy of her turns. The only one clean and unhurt was Billy. His talent didn't hit back! He played the piano and was remarkable at it. He started playing when he was five years old. Sam remembered once when they were all young, the piano teacher walked over to his parents after one of Billy's lessons. He told them, "This child is a prodigy." For weeks after that, Charlie and Sam were careful not to get too close to him. They didn't know if what he had was catching or not. However, Mother was absolutely right about those family dinners. Sam still got a very special feeling throughout his body whenever he thought of those dinner get-togethers.

Despite all the pain and agony, they all did well. Halfway through the football season, they had played six tough teams and beat them all. Also there was talk about Sarah trying out for the Olympic team. Her coach, Ron Gordon, had been an assistant coach with the team for six years prior to coming to Chicago. He thought that she had tremendous ability and the stamina to be a champion. It took four frustrating visits with her mother to finally convince her to allow Sarah to do it.

When baseball season started, Charlie was ready. He told the coach that he had been lifting weights all winter to keep in shape. Sam liked his version better. He thought it had more to do with all the girl s Charlie worked out with. There were so many girls that it was remarkable Charlie was able to keep track of them all.

Mother said this proved he had a good mind and would someday be a genius. The brothers believed in their mother's wisdom but questioned that.

Mother made it mandatory that we all attend the music festival given monthly at the junior high school. As part of the program, it featured a solo by Billy accompanied by the school orchestra. Sam always wondered if it had anything to do with the fact that their father sponsored the program. He had to admit, however, that Billy was good. Everyone enjoyed listening to him play. Billy became a local celebrity at the old age of fourteen.

Sam's senior year was a mixture of beginnings and endings. He was about to complete his primary education with a high scholastic average. He had also maintained a very satisfying record in football, even though he had been beaten up pretty badly in the last few games. The team ended the season winning the divisional title.

Their final game would be for the state championship. They trained every day for a week and rested for two days before the game. Tony Lucci, the coach, wanted to keep Sam out of this one.

He said, "I know this team. They come from a bad town, and for sure they'll be out to get you."

Sam retorted, "It will take a whole damn army to keep me from playing with my team."

On the day of the game, they were ready. "Buster" Larkin, the offensive center, yelled across the locker room, "Let's go, guys. We're the Pistons. We're number one. Let's shove this game up their ass!" With their adrenaline overflowing, they ran onto the field.

Sam's team won the toss and chose to receive. The battle started on the first play. Scott McDonald, the receiver, ran the ball back to the thirty-five yard line, and that's exactly where he was stopped. Three tacklers hit him simultaneously, and three others piled on just for the fun of it. As they untangled the pile, someone deliberately kicked Scott in the groin, and as the tacklers finally arose, he was the only one who didn't get up. Scott was temporarily paralyzed and had to be carried off the field.

The Pistons still had the ball. They didn't huddle but set up immediately to try to get the other team off balance. Buster, who was six foot two and weighed 285 pounds, snapped the ball. He was rushed and flattened as four guys ran over him to get to the quarterback, Chuck Gurney. Chuck managed to pass the ball just before they got to him. Playing dirty, they leveled the empty-handed quarterback anyway.

Sam was off the line on time, ran fifteen yards down the field and turned to receive the ball. Instead he got a stomach full of some enormously fat blocker. It slowed him down enough for two other guys to hit him. As Sam went down, one of them elbowed him in the ribs while the other one slammed his knee into Sam's groin.

The coach was right, he thought. *These guys are crazy.*

As the game progressed, the Pistons managed to put some points on the board. They were ahead by three when the gun fired, ending the first half. The team looked like a stampeding herd of buffalo had run over them as they dragged themselves back to the lockers. The coach was already there and started his pep talk as they came in. The guys were hurting bad. The defensive guys were all chopped up and bleeding.

As they gathered around the ice bucket, Sam overheard one of the team say, "Those bastards are nuts! They keep coming at us with fire in their eyes yelling, 'Get the Jap; get the Jap!' I kept yelling back, 'He's not on defense; he's on offense.'" He turned and smiled at Sam. "Just kidding." Sam knew he was kidding, but he was probably right. Those sons of bitches were looking for a fight, and he was the main target.

The coach looked at his watch. He hesitated for a second as if he was contemplating throwing in the towel. Then he changed his mind. Jumping to his feet, he yelled, "Okay, let's go, you guys. I want some butts for my trophy room. I don't want any of those guys leaving the field in one piece."

As Sam ran by him, the coach grabbed him by his shoulders. "Sorry, kid, not you. You definitely won't survive the second half. Those guys are out to get you."

It took Sam a few seconds to readjust his thoughts. All he had been thinking of was getting back out there. Looking deep into the coach's eyes, Sam told him, "It doesn't matter. If I don't finish it now, I will have to finish it after the game."

The coach grinned at him and said, "You can play under one condition. You bring back that fat bastard's balls. They'll look good on my wall too."

Sam knew that he was referring to the guy who spent most of the first half sitting on his stomach.

The third quarter was a massacre. Their defense was coming apart at the seams. With pure determination, they held on, giving up only three points. When the fourth quarter began, the score was tied ten to ten. The guys tried to protect Sam as best as they could, but he continued to get hammered on every play. Sam knew that his team felt bad, and he loved them for trying. What really infuriated their opponents the most was that he wouldn't stay down.

With fifty-five seconds left in the game, they huddled around the coach as he called the last play. Infuriated, he yelled, "These bastards don't want to play ball. They want to fight. So let's give them one! Meathead, you and the rest of the guys beef up the front line. Sam, Buster will lay back as long as he can. You will run for your life and get as far downfield as you can. When Buster releases the ball, the rest of you will hit whoever's left standing and kick the shit out of them!"

As Buster snapped the ball, he reached out and grabbed two linesmen, slowing them down long enough for Meathead to cut in from the right side and take them out permanently. As Chuck released the ball, the rest of the guys went in fast and hard. You could hear bones snapping in every direction. Sam jumped off the line so fast that he was sure he left before the snap. He took Chuck's advice and ran for his life. He was downfield in no time and was able to turn and watch the play develop. Sam was all alone. Chuck's throw was pure arrogance. It was his way of telling the other team to go to hell. Sam reached out, pulled the ball in, and ran twenty yards for a touchdown.

The stadium exploded with cheers and disbelief. The gun fired, ending the game, and they were the state champs. Sam had mixed emotions. As they ran off the field, he looked back. The injured players of the other team were still lying out there waiting for an empty stretcher. He remembered thinking, *Is this a sign of things to come?*

CHAPTER 6

Breaking into the American automobile market was not going to be easy. In fact it would be virtually impossible. For nearly ten years, Sam's father beat the pavement, going from company to company. Most of them had already made long-term commitments.

The engines and drive shafts they were using had only been developed within the past few years. Even though the manufacturers individually boasted that they had the better one, they actually only varied slightly. No one was ready for any big changes, especially a smaller engine with less power from Japan.

The manufacturers were naturally motivated by profit. They would have to produce many thousands of engines to offset the development costs. In the future it would be referred to as "beating a product to death." The procedure was already antiquated and self-defeating. While waiting for that magical number, they locked themselves into the same product for years. The heads of the automobile conglomerates made it virtually impossible to introduce something new before they were ready or had a need for it.

Fortunately, a need did develop. While American automakers were concentrating on quantity, European manufacturers were concentrating on quality. They outpaced the United States by miles. US automakers were put to shame in almost every form of competitive racing competition.

Racing was in its infancy in America, whereas the Europeans had been promoting it for years. It served two major purposes. Racing provided a grueling cross-country testing ground, and it brought out thousands of spectators, who would eventually become consumers.

By this time, Father's frustration had reached its boiling point. He came to the dinner table one evening and sat down in his regular seat at the head of the table. He reached out for a helping of meat that Mother had just brought to the table and placed it neatly on his plate. Then, with his fork still in his right hand, he reached out and stabbed a baked potato. He announced loudly that he had had enough!

It was time to try something different. He decided that he was going to return to Japan and convince Grandfather that it might be better to produce their own cars. Grandfather Sagarra was good at what he did. More importantly, he was highly respected as a successful businessman, who followed the old Japanese customs and traditions. This made him a leader among his peers.

Father wasn't planning anything big to start with. His plan was more on the line of an experimental laboratory facility. There he could develop and test new vehicles designed to use their own engines and drive shafts. He knew that it wouldn't be easy. Japan was going through its own economic changes, and new ventures in other countries weren't on top of anyone's list of priorities.

CHAPTER 7

It was Sept. 15, 1932, when Father left for Japan. Upon arriving at the airport, he noticed that there were an unusual number of security guards at the reception booths checking new arrivals. Father still had his Japanese passport, which normally would have let him pass right through. Instead he was detained with everyone else and had to open all of his luggage. Security was very thorough. They searched through everything and finally gave him the okay to leave. He gathered his belongings and headed toward the exit, where he was met by Grandfather's chauffeur, Tai.

Father recognized him immediately, even though he hadn't seen him for years. Tai had been with Grandfather for many years. The two men walked toward each other. Tai hesitated, smiled, and bowed. As Father got close enough, Tai reached out to relieve him of his suitcases. As their hands touched, Father resisted for a split second. He almost forgot that he was back home and it would be a great embarrassment for him, being part of the upper class, to carry his own baggage.

Grandfather's home was in a uniquely defined upper-class area of gently rolling hills. His home was large, but there were many that were larger. What made his home impressive was the location. It was built on top of the hill so Grandfather could look down on the city of Tokyo.

Sam could remember Father describing his feeling of excitement and the childhood memories that came flooding back to him as the house came into view. As the car stopped, the front doors to the house were thrown open. As Father got out of the car, he was instantly filled with joy. He recognized the woman who was waiting to greet him. "Meilee, Meilee," he shouted as he threw his arms around her neck and held her close for a few seconds, completely forgetting everything he had ever learned about Japanese customs.

As he regained control of his emotions, he quickly let her go and stepped back. He bowed his head to her, asking for her forgiveness. "Too many years away have dulled my memory of our customs," he said.

With a smile she slowly bowed her head. She said, "If that was a traditional American greeting, I suggest a little more restraint when you greet your father." She gently turned away from him, and with her left hand gently motioned for him to follow her. "I will bring you to your father."

As they walked through the house, each room brought back a special memory of a joyous event or ritual that would ignite and mystify a child's imagination.

Grandfather had been expecting him and was waiting for him in his quarters. This was a private part of the house that was strictly off limits to anyone without a special invitation. It was a complex of lounging areas, conference rooms, a large dining facility, and Grandfather's private office. It was not uncommon to see geisha girls scurrying around the complex. Grandfather enjoyed their company, and he was sure that they kept his associates in a pleasant frame of mind. It helped them to make favorable decisions when they got together for an important meeting. The geisha girls were exceedingly beneficial on occasions when an impasse was encountered. They would quickly bring out the sake and smooth out the ripples.

Grandfather enjoyed his geisha girls and loved his sake. Father always believed that the combination of the two was probably one of the main reasons for his success. He explained that this was his therapy to remove anxiety. Men without anxiety have clear minds, and clear minds can make decisions. Good or bad, they made decisions. Their success was measured by their percentage of good decisions. Fortunately, Grandfather's percentage was extremely high.

As Meilee rolled back the large doors of the private lounge, Grandfather was standing next to a large, glass-enclosed porcelain statue that was hundreds of years old. As he turned to face Father, both of them locked eyes in a warm, emotional embrace. Both of the men, without touching, were able to feel each other's heart beating.

Grandfather approached and said, "Son, you look well, and I am pleased to see you have arrived safely."

The years spent apart seemed to fade away. They had a lot to talk about and some very important decisions to make.

A few days went by before Father spoke about the purpose of his visit home. His idea of starting a plant in the United States to design and build cars for Americans wasn't going to be easy to get approved. A proposal of this magnitude was going to be extremely risky. To play it safe, he knew that Grandfather would want to bring in the entire consortium. Father knew that he had to have Grandfather's support The consortium would not make a move without Grandfather's stamp of approval. Father had to get him to believe in his concept.

Grandfather arranged to have the consortium meet at his house. He told Father that he was expected to address the members. The burden of convincing them to participate in this venture would be entirely his. "It's time that you feel what it's like to be in control, how good it feels when everything goes along smoothly. And when things don't go smoothly, you feel as though you were being kicked in the groin by a water buffalo."

The arrangements were quite elaborate. This was to be Father's first appearance before the entire membership. Grandfather wanted it to be a memorable one. As it turned out, he really did not have to worry about that. Father presented his idea of starting a plant in the United States, and the unanimous consensus was that he had lost his mind.

However, this was only the first round. Grandfather suggested a recess. He raised his arm as though it was a magic wand. Geisha girls, carrying trays of refreshments, scurried out of every corner of the room. When the trays were emptied, they returned with sake. Grandfather's technique of wining and dining the consortium was in high gear.

When they finally got back to business, Father was surprised to see that no one had gone. Everyone had returned to his place. Obviously, Grandfather's plan had worked. Father soon realized that keeping the members together was easier than putting out the fire in their heads. The refreshments and sake did nothing to change their minds concerning his sanity.

The questions started coming at him like kamikazes. Kiyoshi Masuda, a heavyset man with a pudgy face, asked, "Why would we want to risk so much to start an entire new design and production facility in a foreign land? I think it would undermine our productivity here at home. It would be counter-productive and put our own people out of work. Besides, I don't believe that Americans will ever aggressively buy Japanese products, especially our smaller-designed cars."

Father explained that he did not think his idea would be counter-productive. In fact, he was sure it would even create more work for the Japanese people. He zeroed in on the fact that all he wanted to do was to start a design and technological facility. He wanted to utilize America's advanced technology and apply it to his designs. This way he would shorten the time it took to produce the final product, a product that would be tailored for the American market rather than the Japanese market.

Father's ideas were visionary, and he was way ahead of the times. After the war, however, Father would be proven right. Japan's entire wartime industrialization would be converted to produce products tailored for the American consumer. As time passed, they would become experts at it.

Meanwhile, back at the meeting, the kamikazes kept coming, but Father kept his cool. Fortunately, he was a patient man with a high level of tolerance. His attributes were shown by the amount of years he spent in America trying to develop a successful business. He kept his composure as he methodically weighed each question. He had to be sure his answers were definite, without the slightest degree of uncertainty in his voice.

As the hours went by, the questions became less critical. It was as though everyone was becoming hypnotized one by one they settled back in their chairs. Suddenly there was complete silence. The silence was more frightening than the chaos that had transpired beforehand.

Kei thought surely he had destroyed what he came for and disgraced his father. That would have been worse than death itself.

As he looked around the table, he was positive this was the end. It seemed as though everyone had closed their eyes and had actually fallen asleep. Father was contemplating *seppuku*, better known as *hara-kiri*, when miraculously the gods, who obviously didn't want to deal with a messy seppuku, brought the board back to life.

One by one they began to open their eyes and heads started to nod. Soon the entire membership was nodding. Father curiously looked at Grandfather, who was smiling from ear to ear. This apparently was the membership's sign of approval. Father had done it! It was a unanimous approval, the first one since the beginning of the consortium. Grandfather and Father were filled with joy at this accomplishment.

Later on, when they were finally alone, Father expressed his fear that he had put the board to sleep. Grandfather softly replied, "Sake." He finally realized that this was all part of a well-orchestrated plan to get his ideas approved. It was put together by Grandfather, the old professional.

CHAPTER 8

Back in Chicago, with the funding he needed, Father located a vacant two-story building that had previously been used to repair large trucks in the south end of town. Overshadowed by much larger buildings that had been built around the turn of the century, it was tucked in as though it was meant to be a hiding place.

Father always told us that we didn't have to worry about the security of the building because the landlord was Al Capone. We never knew if he was kidding or not because ·the old place did smell like a brewery. Sam always had this picture in his mind of two hoods, packing .38s, coming to collect the rent.

The building was old, but it was built to last a hundred years. It looked as though its time had come and gone. However, Father thought the building would be perfectly suited to construct engines. There were two floors. The downstairs would be ideal for construction and assembly while the upstairs could be used as an office and laboratory. Most importantly, it would be where the design and testing of the new engines could be carried out. There was only one entrance and exit, making it easy to maintain privacy and security.

The funding from the consortium was deposited in Chicago National Fidelity, one of the leading banks of that time. It was helpful that the bank's corporate executive officer was Jack McGovern, the Sagarras' next-door neighbor. For the first time in almost ten years, grandfather formally acknowledged the fact that we were truly an American representation of the Sagarra family.

Sam was a close friend of the banker's son, Tom, and his daughter, Margaret (everyone had called her Mickey as far back as Sam could remember). The family had only now become somewhat "acceptable" and had advanced a few notches in status. Instead of referring to them as the Japanese, they were now referred to as the "rich Japs."

Jack McGovern was an opportunist. He had been named CEO of the bank five years earlier. At the time, a deal came across his desk that involved a company that was wildcatting for oil. The company also had interests in gold mine claims. As the story went, it was acquired by extremely unethical tactics. As luck would have it, the company struck oil and the first mine it excavated became one of the richest gold strikes of its time. For lending the company most of the money they needed to get started, McGovern negotiated and received for the bank a one-third interest in the company. From then on, it was like being on a shooting star. Most of the deals he made were risky and wouldn't be touched by other banks. McGovern's motto was "I throw twelve deals up in the air every month. If half of them materialize, then I'm a winner." As his luck was going, he threw up twelve and twelve materialized. He was clearly a brilliant risk-taker.

Before McGovern would throw his weight, all 280 pounds of it, and the bank's money behind anyone, he had to be convinced that the person could deliver. He loved a challenge. The risk and the reward were there. However, it was the uniqueness of the challenge that aroused his interest. A Jap that was going to make a bigger and better engine for Americans in Chicago was definitely a challenge Jack McGovern was interested in.

McGovern would become the most influential factor in Father's drive toward success. He knew a lot of people and had good contacts in the business community. If, by chance, he didn't know an influential contact, he knew someone who did. Once McGovern committed to a project, success was the most important factor. His philosophy was that winning penetrated all barriers—race, color, and religion. It all came under one heading: victory. He always preached, "If you have a good idea, try it before someone else does."

With McGovern's help, Father was able to get all the contractors he needed to set up the plant. It was ready to go within six months. McGovern was also influential in convincing some of the top technicians from the major auto manufacturers to join Father's company. When Sam thought about it, it probably wasn't as difficult as McGovern made it seem. Most of the manufacturers at that time were bogged down. They would not start pumping out large amounts of cash for research and development until the existing systems had paid for themselves. Most of the innovative technicians had been put out to pasture. When McGovern called, Father had the pick of the crop, and he took the cream right off the top. The guys were full of ideas about how to build bigger and better engines. Father was no slouch either. He had attended the best technological college in Japan. When he graduated, not only was he at the top of the class but he also was individually honored for his advanced theories and creative ability.

One of the first technicians to join the company was a lanky fellow named Jim McBride. He had long arms with large hands. Sam remembered him the most because he had never seen anyone with such large hands. He couldn't imagine Jim holding a pen or a pencil unless they were custom made for him. As time went by, those hands would become magic wands. Not only could they design but they also could build, and build they did! He would become Father's most valuable asset and good friend.

The next man on board was Robbie Kantor, a compression expert. He was medium height with curly red hair and always seemed to be in a good mood. Except for a scar across the right side of his face, which he jokingly referred to as "the result of too much pressure," Robbie was a good-looking guy.

Marty Bradshaw was an aspiring engineer fresh out of college. Father wanted him because Marty reminded him of himself. Marty was bright with a head full of new ideas and concepts. When he spoke, it seemed as though he couldn't get the words out fast enough. His mind churned out so many ideas so quickly. The part of the brain responsible for speech found it difficult to keep up with the demand.

Jack McGovern recommended Terry Woodward. Sam and Charlie thought that she was a spy for McGovern, someone to keep him abreast of what was happening or give him a progress report once in a while. Father never agreed with them. He always said, "Anyone that pretty couldn't be a spy."

Father was always governed by beauty, whether it was human or mechanical. As it turned out, he was right. She became an important part of the team and would prove her loyalty many times over.

The team was coming together better than anyone had expected. The talent that was out there in suspended animation was unbelievable. Everyone's spirits were as high as the stars. Father was off and running. He named the company Chicago Motors Incorporated (CMI) No one believed more in our ability to get it together than Jack McGovern. For him it was payback time; despite all the success he had achieved for the bank, the automobile market had always eluded him.

The automobile manufacturers had shunned him. They considered McGovern and the bank too speculative for their comfort. Jack would continually ridicule them. "Who ever said making a lot of money was supposed to be comfortable?" The biggest rewards always came from the highest risks, and so far he was batting a thousand.

Watching guys like Marty, Robbie, and Jim working together, shooting questions and answers at each other, and witnessing the ideas become working steel components and eventually the creation of a powerful engine was mind-boggling to us. It stretched our imaginations beyond reality.

It was good experience because what we learned from those guys was that life is like a dream. The dream creates a need, and a need creates a challenge to create a method to satisfy that need. As long as visionary man can dream, the cycle will continue like perpetual motion. There will be no limit to what man can create. This thought would stay with Sam for the rest of his life, and it would come to the surface many times.

Sam would never forget the first test he observed. The place was buzzing with excitement. It was the first engine Marty and Robbie had completed. It was a new design with a different shape. It looked slightly oval. Due to its shape, a thousand pages of theory and calculation said it would deliver more horsepower with less stress on the pistons. It would also be more economical to operate. The components were tested separately throughout the year. All parts passed with flying colors.

This was the first time that all the components were assembled and would be tested together as an engine. As the anticipation reached the boiling point, everything was finally ready to go. The door was closed, leaving the engine isolated in the room resting on a wooden support. Everyone watched from the special viewing portals surrounding the room.

Robbie was given the honor to push the button for the first test. As he put his thumb on the button, he hesitated just for a second. Then he pushed it down all the way. The engine roared to a start. Everyone could feel the excitement running through their bodies. Hand shaking and congratulations had already started when suddenly the engine burst into flames and blew into a thousand pieces. The excitement quickly changed to sudden shock and disbelief. For ten minutes, the engine ran beautifully. Then, without any warning, it exploded.

Father was the first to regain his composure. He walked slowly toward the closed door of the testing room. When he opened it, smoke came billowing out. After it finally cleared, they all filed in to get a better look at what had occurred. It was gone! How could the entire engine just burn up? The only thing left was the charred remains of the wooden support that it had been resting on.

Marty was the first one to speak. He said, "It was going great. Everything was in sync and running smoothly. It had to be the compression. We'll have to beef up the steel."

Robby looked at him and said, "I think you're right. I'd like to put this one back together again."

Marty turned slowly and looked into Robbie's eyes. "You must have been in here when this thing blew up and got hit in the head. Look around you. There must be a thousand pieces of steel imbedded in the walls and ceiling. They'll be sending rocket ships to the moon by the time we figure out where all these pieces go."

Robbie started laughing as did everyone else. They knew Marty was joking, trying to make the best of a disappointing situation. Jim McBride looked at us and just shrugged his large shoulders.

CMI had now been in operation for a few years, and the results of everyone's hard labor were apparently about to pay off. The plant seemed to be full of anxiety, as though something was about to happen. Sam learned later on that Marty Bradshaw and some new guy they hired—Jack Morrison, a metallurgist—were testing a new metal. This new composition would be a mixture of the old steel, which was utilized by the entire industry at that time, and a much lighter steel component. This new reversion would produce an engine with high compression, deliver 40 percentage more horsepower and would weigh one-third less than the engines already in production.

The testing day finally arrived. All the final preparations had been completed. The engine was mounted on a stationary chassis. The test chamber was closed off on all sides. The wall had small clear panels that allowed everyone to observe the test. No one really knew what to expect. With all these geniuses and their calculations, it would be the engine that would have the last word. And that it did!

Everything went okay when Marty pushed the button to start her up. The engine kicked over immediately, which was a good sign. In previous tests of other engines, it usually required a preparatory period to get the fuel flowing through the lines. Then, once the engines had started, they idled roughly until the valves were adjusted.

This time, however, the engine started instantly, an excellent sign that everything was synchronized. The new metal and the newly designed components were performing according to everyone's expectations and might even be exceeding them.

Marty Bradshaw called out to Robbie Kantor, "Heat is holding at normal; cooling system is working fine."

Robbie called back, "Oil pressure is good and holding. Let's open her up and see where she goes." He wanted to test the marriage of the new metals.

As the pressure increased, pushing the engine beyond their calculations, they were overjoyed at their apparent success. Suddenly there was a loud explosion, and the ceiling of the test chamber seemed to disappear. They realized they had pushed it way too far. An eerie silence crept through the plant.

Then, what seemed to be an hour later but was no more than about thirty seconds, Robbie looked across the room at Marty. Marty turned to look at Father. Simultaneously, they all focused in on Jack Morrison and broke into wild laughter. Father paused long enough to take a deep breath and yell across to Morrison, "This was one marriage pushed beyond its limits." The truth was they had a very good engine. The test was a success. A slight modification was needed to reinforce the head and strengthen the marriage. Then the engine would be ready to go into a full program of road testing.

The new engine was christened the "CMlOl." It was time to test it outdoors. They had installed the engine into a standard four-door sedan. After the engine had passed all the laboratory tests with flying colors, they wanted to see how it would react to pushing some weight. However, there was one big problem. CMI didn't have a facility of its own to do the type of road testing required to prove CMlOl's ability to perform. They would need a track large enough to create on- and off-road conditions, and one that would be secure from spectators or spies.

For this task, Father again turned to his old friend Jack McGovern. McGovern had been waiting for this day as eagerly as anyone at CM I. He wanted to have a personal hand in helping something successful come to life. He told Father about a racetrack two miles outside the city. The owners of the track had recently come to him to borrow money for a major renovation. McGovern thought that in its rundown state and natural hazardous conditions, it might be exactly what Father was looking for without having to spend a lot of money. Father thought it was a good idea. He asked Jim McBride and Robbie Kantor to check out the track. They returned with a good report. The track was broken up enough to simulate off-road conditions, and it had a long enough run of good pavement to do the other required tests. In essence, the track was perfect.

Now it was up to Jack McGovern. All he had to do was convince the present owner to let CMI use the track long enough to complete its testing of CMlOl. Jack knew that if CM101 was successful, they could build their own track and he would have played a major role in it. He had no problem with the present owners. All he had to do was promise them the money for the refurbishing and they gave CMI the place, lock, stock and barrel for six months.

The team got started immediately. Marty, Robbie, and Jim worked day and night to get everything prepared. Within sixty days, they were on the track and going strong. They enlisted the services of Ray Palma, one of the best test drivers of his time. With his help they devised tests no one had dreamed of as yet. For the next few months, they kept pushing CM101 to the limit, and it kept on performing superbly. They kept at it until they exhausted every part of their imagination to create a new obstacle. CM101 proved to be an amazing innovation. It was, without a doubt, a winner!

Unfortunately, as feared, the eyes of CMI weren't the only eyes observing the tests. When someone comes up with something that amazing, word manages to leak out. It was a risk they had to take. Shortly after the testing, Father was contacted by a man named Roger Dawson, who represented a group of investors. They were interested in CMI's new engine.

Father curiously asked, "How could anyone be interested in something that hasn't been made public yet?"

Dawson replied, "That's my business. That's what I get paid for: finding out about things like this before they become public. Right now I have some people who want your engine. In fact, they would be willing to buy the whole company for a price I'm positive you would be very satisfied with."

Father's reply was short and polite. "I'm sorry, Mr. Dawson, but we plan to produce the engine ourselves, and CMI is not for sale."

By 1940 the company was in high gear. Despite Japan's extremely worsening relationship with America, Jack McGovern was able to convince the bank to lend Father the money to revamp the entire building, making it a full-production facility for CM101. The Japanese government was now being run by the military, which passed a law forbidding the transfer of any funds to America.

This new law left Father stranded just when it seemed he had succeeded. Jack McGovern's loan was more than helpful in saving CMI. Once again he had displayed his faith in Father. A few weeks later, in a confidential conversation, the two men expressed their concerns to each other. The progressively deteriorating relations with Japan were turning sentiment against Japanese Americans. Jack expressed his concern to Father. "Americans could be fighting Japanese in the Pacific, but here in America they'll be fighting you."

Despite all the agitation, CMI was going ahead with its plan to produce the engine. The team's determination to make CM101 a reality was all Father needed to keep going. Roger Dawson kept up a continual barrage of calls, trying to convince him to sell the company. There was also a new caller who would not give his name. He demanded that Father give up the idea of producing the new engine. "Be smart. Sell out. Take the money and run before there's nothing to sell and you'll have to run anyway," he threatened.

There were other threats as well. Father just shrugged them off as cranks and kept the calls to himself.

CHAPTER 9

Tom McGovern and Sam had played football together for many years. Tom was always there to throw a block for Sam when he needed it most. He was the most important factor in Sam's coming out of each game in one piece. Tom had become his closest and dearest friend. Together, they had planned for years to join Father's company. By the time the plant was in full swing, they were in their senior year.

They both loved cars and engines. Both of them had attended special courses at their high school taught by professional engineers. There was a small two-story building at the back of our property that must have originally been used as a guesthouse. Tom and Sam converted the first floor into a workshop. The top floor was a two-room apartment that they set up as a private club. They had seven regular members, including Tom, Sam, and Tom's sister, Mickey. She ran the place. If anyone got out of line, her Irish temper would flare up, and she'd bust him or her in the mouth.

Sam remembered one evening when a few members of the football team had come by to celebrate beating a tough team earlier that day. Everything was going along fine. They had all brought their girlfriends, except for Meathead Baker. The phonograph was playing romantic music. Some of the kids were dancing, and the rest were in the other room on the couch or the bed.

Mickey felt that temperatures were going too high though, so she politely announced, "It's time for everyone to leave."

Reluctantly, they said good night and started walking out the door, except for Meathead. As he walked by Mickey, he said, "Good night, sweetie," and patted her on the ass. With one violent, revolving motion, her long red hair flying wildly and her Irish green eyes on fire, she hit him across the face with the back of her hand. Simultaneously she kicked him in the butt, causing this huge hulk of a football player to fall down the full flight of stairs. As he lay there in agony, she yelled down at him, "Next time I'll knock your fat meathead off and stick it up your ass."

It was hilarious. He lay there writhing in pain, and we all couldn't stop laughing. Fortunately for the team, he only wound up with a few superficial bruises. She was great, and Sam loved her from that moment on. Mickey became their constant companion. She loved cars and racing as much as they did, and she could adjust a valve or change a tire as fast as anyone of them.

Sam remembered the first time he kissed her. He had gotten out of school early one day. It was a hot and muggy morning, and he was working under the hood with his shirt off. One of the distributor wires was twisted and sparking, which caused the engine to idle roughly. Mickey sneaked up behind him and grabbed his ribs with both hands, intending to scare him.

Sam accidentally touched the sparking distributor wires, and they both lit up. He spun around in fright. The shock of being hit from the front and simultaneously being grabbed from behind was one hell of a feeling for the both of them.

There she was with her long, wavy red hair in her face, her beautiful green eyes tearing up, and her mouth frozen slightly open. Sam reached out, put his hands on her waist, pulled her toward him, and kissed her. As their bodies touched, he could feel Mickey's heart pounding. She put her arms around his neck, and they stood there wrapped in a close embrace. She was wearing a cropped blouse that just covered her breasts, leaving her middle exposed.

Mickey felt warm and smooth in his arms. Sam could have held her forever. As she pulled her head back and smiled, he kissed her again. When they finally separated, both of them started laughing uncontrollably. The reason she had felt so smooth to him was because his hands and arms were full of grease. She was covered with the stuff.

"Sam, I love you," she said, "but you will have to help me scrub this grease off. I can't walk out of here looking like this." Although she had spent a lot of hours in the shop with them, she'd have a hell of a time explaining how the grease got up her back and over her shoulders from behind.

From that time on the clubhouse became their private hideaway. Living next door to each other was a blessing. They would wait until everyone had gone to bed. Then the two of them would sneak out and spend half the night in the apartment. Curled up on the couch together, they kissed and held each other while they talked about the future. They shared many of their personal and secret feelings. She was the only one he told about his love for flying and the sea, and how both represented a feeling of freedom and adventure to him.

Sam told her about his plan to join the naval air force after graduation. That way he'd be able to get the best of both worlds—the sea and the air—while acquiring enough technological training to join his father's business later on. He had never shared his feelings with anyone else before. Mickey told him about her plan to attend college with biology as her major.

They always took the precaution of setting a small alarm clock in case they fell asleep, though it really wasn't necessary. They always seemed to have so much to talk about that they never did fall asleep. Somehow Sam and Mickey managed to keep a lid on their emotions before they lost control.

CHAPTER 10

RACING HAD BECOME AN important part of their lives. For some of the guys, it became a passion. Even though the auto industry was in its infancy, it had enough appeal to ignite their imaginations—imaginations that were not inhibited by the need to show a profit.

They would take cars that were put together by an assembly line, cut down the bodies and rebuild the engines. The end result produced more power and speed. Their imagination and ingenuity took the industry to the cutting edge of its technology, leading the way for the manufacturers to follow. Fortunately for the auto industry, many of these young innovators would become their future top executives.

The sport of racing tested their ability and created a need. This need ignited their imaginations to go further, further than anyone had ever gone before. That's how the industry was born and hopefully would be kept alive. There were clubs forming all over the state. Some of the "old crust" called them gangs, but mostly they were just regular kids. The cars provided a perfect outlet for them to express themselves. Each car reflected the individual personality of its owner.

Sam and Tom named their club the Road Blazers. For them it was now close to payoff time. They had purchased a few cars and raced them throughout the years. Most wound up with blown engines or broken drive shafts. The rules in those early days were a little vague. The way some of the guys drove, you would have believed the rules were written in a foreign language. The majority of the time the cars wound up as wrecks.

After almost a year, the newest club creation was completed and being prepared for testing. The car was a conglomeration of all their ideas. Having access to a technical facility like CMI gave them a definite edge. Number one on the list of advantages was Jim McBride, their good friend and advisor.

Building the car was the culmination of a year's hard work by Tom, Sam, and two other members of the club, Jerry Burke and Larry Bogart. They had all donated whatever they could. Coupled with the technical assistance of Jim McBride and Robbie Kantor of CMI, they now had the Road Blazers' #1 ready to go. Having a father in the automobile business gave Sam a definite advantage.

They took the car to an abandoned airfield where most of the local races were held. For about an hour or so, they tested their new car. Except for stopping twice to make a few minor adjustments, the car performed perfectly. They were all jubilant over Number One's performance. Everyone yelled, "Let's go for the two hundred!"

The two hundred was a new race arranged by a few local sportsmen in an effort to keep up with the Europeans. It was a grueling two hundred miles of crossing back country roads and small towns. The course not only tested the car's durability but also the experience and the guts of the drivers.

The race was only a week away when Sam and Tom finished their final preparations. Pit stops were arranged at approximately fifty-mile intervals. Mickey, Jerry Burke, and Larry Bogart would be their service mechanics.

The cross-country race would be on the open road. Never having been in a race of this sort, they were not prepared for what lay ahead. Both of them decided that Sam would drive the first fifty miles and Tom would navigate. They arrived at that decision because Tom was more familiar with the country surrounding the first leg of the race. After that, it didn't make a difference who drove or navigated because neither one of them knew where they were going.

The day of the race was overcast and drizzling. The forecast was for rain, but nothing could dampen their spirits. All of the cars were at the starting line and took off on time. There were twenty-four cars in all, and Sam and Tom were in the tenth position. Jerry Burke, Larry Bogart, and Mickey had gone ahead to the prearranged stops designated for refueling and repairs. They would be waiting if and when Blazer #1 arrived.

By the time they completed the first fifty miles, the new drivers knew exactly what was meant when they said "cross-country." They went through eighteen small towns connected by a maze of one-lane, paved or partially paved roads. Usually that meant a layer of stone that was saturated in a heavy oil and asphalt mixture to keep the stones from being picked up by the rear wheels. Otherwise, the car in front could propel the stones like little meteors to the car behind. The cars they drove had no tops, and Sam and Tom only wore goggles to protect their eyes from the elements. So the "meteors" became a particular hazard. Having one bounce off your head was a painful and messy situation.

The part of the race that Sam would remember best was when the road crisscrossed through the back farm country. Those roads were completely unpaved. Depending on the weather, they were dry and dusty or wet and muddy with ten-inch ruts. Occasionally the drivers would encounter a bunch of cows being led by a farmer who was unaware of the race or just didn't care. They would have to come to a crawl until the herd got out of the way.

Another important lesson the novice racers learned in their first race was position. Normally in a race, the driver's position was picked out of a hat. When you have twenty or thirty cars participating, everyone can't be first. It becomes the luck of the draw. When the starting position is far back, the driver's ability and experience are tested the most. A driver who started buried in the pack could potentially wind up crossing the finish line first.

The drivers completed their first fifty-mile stretch slightly behind schedule. The first leg had taken them through four small towns, whose connecting roads were paved. Each town had a special greeting for them. Everyone was treating the race as though it was a county fair, so the streets were crowded with residents. As they drove into town, people ran out onto the course and surrounded their cars. They had to slow down to a standstill as the well-wishers placed packages of food and candy into their cars. Some of the onlookers didn't understand what the spectacle was all about. Cross-country racing was still so new.

As Sam and Tom pulled into the first of their four prearranged pit stops, Mickey and the guys were waiting. As Sam got out, Mickey threw her arms around his neck and gave him a big kiss. Suddenly she pulled away, smacking her lips.

She asked curiously, "Okay, Sam, where have you guys been?"

He laughingly replied, "You're tasting cotton candy. Some lady almost shoved it down my throat. That last town had one hell of a party waiting for us."

Mickey, looking at her watch, snapped back, "Yeah, it sure looks like you helped them celebrate." The guys were just closing the hood when she yelled, "Okay, let's get these speed demons out of here." As they sped off, Mickey screamed at the top of her lungs, "And don't stop for any cotton candy."

Sam and Tom had been fortunate so far because the roads between the towns on their first fifty miles were paved and fairly decent. The second stretch would take them into the back farm country. Tom was driving, and it had started to rain. Within the first four miles, they passed a car that was wrapped around a huge oak tree. Later on they learned that the driver had swerved to avoid hitting a dog. The dog, unnerved by the unusual noise of the hot rod, had shot out of a hidden driveway to attack the car as it drove by.

The rain was coming down a little heavier now, and the roads were becoming muddy. The car in front of them tried slowing down as he approached a curve. He hit the brakes and went careening sideways into some farmer's cornfield. When the driver regained control of his car, he drove around in circles, trying to find his way back to the road. The farmer thought that the man was trying to demolish his cornfield and fired buckshot at the bewildered driver, who was delighted to escape with his hide intact.

Blazer #1 was doing its own share of slipping and sliding, but Tom managed to keep the car on the road. Their luck was holding out so far. With help from Mother Nature, the race had certainly not been boring. She had presented them with a deluge of rain that turned the dirt roads into seas of mud. Two other cars they had passed were stuck in ruts so large, they looked like trenches filled with water. Tom and Sam had to navigate their way through the woods to get around those disasters.

Another driver had crashed into the broad side of a barn for no apparent reason. There was loud cheering from the crowds lining the road ahead. The people dodged out of the way to avoid being hit as the car raced by. The roar of the crowd signified that Sam and Tom were in third position with the leaders only about a mile ahead of them. Filled with excitement, Sam yelled across to Tom, "We've almost got them now. Let's show them what this car is made of. Step on it!"

They apparently had made the correct choice. Tom was a great driver in inclement weather. He belonged to a voluntary snow-removal brigade that cleared the streets for churches and other charitable organizations. He always made sure that he drove the plow. The worse the weather, the more Tom liked it.

However, there is a distinct difference between plowing snow and racing in mud. Snow is usually clean and can be easily brushed away while the mud from those back roads adhered to everything. It covered the windshield and their goggles like gooey, heavy molasses. They carried some wet towels for the sole purpose of wiping off mud. One of the navigator's most important jobs was to make sure a towel was always in readiness. The driver had to have clean goggles to keep the car from going off the road.

As they drove into the next town, the two leading cars were in sight. Sam could feel the excitement building in Tom as his foot pushed the accelerator pedal to the floor. The engine began to roar. Tom yelled, "Sam, we've got them now." They were closing in fast when all of a sudden the car in front of them started slowing down. The mud was so thick that they could hardly see the car's brake lights go on.

Sam had to scream over the roar of the engine. "What is happening?"

Tom shrugged his shoulders and said, "Don't know. I can't see a thing. Give me the rag."

Sam quickly handed the towel to Tom so he could wipe the muck from his goggles.

Still screaming at him, Sam asked, "Do you think he's having engine trouble?"

Tom threw the towel back to him and yelled, "No, the car in front of him is slowing down also." As they got closer, he yelled out, "It looks like there's a couple of horses pulling a hay wagon in front of him."

The leader of the race was unable to pass because the wagon was so wide that it blocked the entire road. They had all closed ranks, driving behind one another at a snail's pace. A feeling of exaltation came over Sam and Tom. They knew that once that hay wagon turned off the road, they had the power to pass the two guys leading the pack. Sam said happily, "We'll let them eat our mud for the rest of the race." Unfortunately, that didn't happen too quickly. It seemed that the farmer still had quite a long way to go. Sam told them later, "It was like following Hannibal and his elephants."

They soon realized why Hannibal carried a shovel. With the mud continually showering them, they slowly proceeded. The wheels of the first car flung the mud back to the second car. The second car followed suit, and everyone was saturated with it.

However, this time it wasn't only mud. Tom wrinkled up his nose and yelled at Sam, "What the hell is this stuff? It ain't chocolate pudding."

It was, in fact, a mixture of mud and horse manure. From the way they smelled, it was mostly the latter. This was a disgusting development. They were caught in a deluge of manure, and both of them were covered with the stuff.

Without any warning, the wagon made a sharp right turn and disappeared. The road was clear and open ahead of them, but they couldn't see it. Sam tried to wipe his goggles and handed the towel to Tom. Everything was covered with the putrid, smelly mess.

Tom stormed out of the car and pulled his goggles off. He yelled, "Holy shit!"

Sam yelled back, "Is that what this stuff is?"

Both men decided afterward that the episode eventually proved lucky for them. The two drivers in front of them were devastated and couldn't get their act together. Tom and Sam took the lead easily.

When they arrived at their next rendezvous point, Mickey and the guys came running to greet them. As they got close, all three suddenly put on the brakes and simultaneously exclaimed, "Holy shit!"

Mickey said, "You guys are full of surprises. What did you do now, attend a party thrown by the three little pigs?"

They all collapsed, convulsed with laughter. This time Sam didn't get any kisses. Mickey stayed far away from him. Then, as the mechanics quickly finished with their minor repairs to the Blazer, she yelled out, "The car's okay. Let's get these porkers back on the road."

Once again Blazer #1 was off and running. Sam and Tom were in the lead and held it for the rest of the race. As they got close to the finish line, the wind was behind them, and their aroma crossed the line ahead of them. Everyone kept looking around as though they were expecting a herd of cattle to suddenly appear.

When it was time for the organizers of the race to present them with their trophy, there was an understandably large distance between the winners and the sponsors as the presentation was made. It didn't matter. They had won, and to Sam and Tom, that was the sweet smell of success.

CHAPTER 11

A FEW WEEKS HAD gone by, and they were still celebrating. Winning the cross-country had put all of them in the limelight. Invitations for future races were coming in from everywhere. The group seemed to be zeroing in on one race in particular: a 250-mile sportsman's endurance race called the Marshall Whitney Cup. The race was named for the sponsor, a local industrialist. It would be run on a paved oval track with thousands of spectators behind a fence that separated them from the cars. This race would be under strict supervision, a complete reversal from the cross-country grand prix they had just won.

The Marshall Whitney Cup was only six weeks off. If they were going to make it, there was still a lot of work ahead of them. The engine they used for the cross-country race was perfect, but the body of the car would be too heavy to obtain the speed required. Speedway racing on a paved track brought out a whole new breed of drivers. Those guys weren't Wild West cowboy drivers. They were daredevil speed demons. If you wanted to race with them, you had to learn to think like them.

Jerry Burke and Larry Bogart had cars of their own that were much lighter than Blazer #1; however, Tom and Sam had a sentimental attachment to their first winning car. They all agreed that if the Blazer's body could be modified in time, they would enter the race as a three-car trio. The prize money would be divided equally, no matter who won.

To reduce the car's weight, they took off everything that was not absolutely essential. When they were finished, the car looked like a chicken without feathers that could fly. They had reduced the Blazer's weight by almost a third. That gave them an oversized, supercharged engine in a light tactile body. It gave a driver the feeling of sitting on a rocket when the accelerator was hit. Tom and Sam were ready with a week to spare, which was perfect timing.

Mickey's prom was two days before the race. She and Sam had spent a lot of time working on the car together. The year had been a busy one for both of them. Sam had been occupied with his racing while Mickey prepared for her graduation and prom. With all this activity, there still weren't any cobwebs hanging in their clubhouse hideaway. Somehow the two of them always managed to squeeze in a little time for themselves.

There seemed to be more for them to talk about than ever. They loved talking and sharing special moments. Mickey told Sam, "Mom said that as long as I keep on talking, I'll be all right." They listened to one another with all the intensity of young love. Communication was the right sort of diversion that kept their emotions under control. It was similar to an extinguisher, whose stream puts the fire out.

Three days before the prom, Mickey called Sam and said, "Please drive me to the store to do some last-minute shopping."

"I'd be happy to," he said. "I'll pick you up in a few minutes."

On the way into town, Mickey yelled suddenly, "Stop! Stop the car!"

Slamming on the brakes in a state of shock, Sam turned to her and said, "What happened? Did we hit something?"

She took a deep breath and hesitated before answering. There was no answer, just complete silence. Sam looked at her as though she had suddenly lost her mind.

Once again he inquired, "Mickey, what happened? Why did you want me to stop the car?"

She turned to him and in a soft voice, said, "You were going too fast, and I didn't want you to miss the next right turn."

He took a quick look up ahead to see if he could figure out what she meant. He was totally bewildered. "What turn? Town is three miles straight ahead." The only turn Sam could see led to a heavily wooded area that the locals called "Lover's Lane." Turning back to her, he said, "You have just given me a perfect example of instant insanity. All the years we've gone together, you have never wanted to go anywhere near that place."

Cutting him short, Mickey defiantly said, "Tonight I do!"

Afraid to ask any more questions, Sam took his foot off the brake and made a right turn. He drove into a clearing, stopped the car, and hesitantly turned off the ignition.

In the darkness he could sense Mickey's apprehension. Sliding over a little closer to her, Sam calmly asked, "What's this all about?"

In a low, steady but determined voice, she said, "This is exactly what I don't want it to be like."

"Like what?" he asked.

Becoming a little angry, she snapped, "Like this!"

Sam started losing his patience but continued questioning her. "Okay, Mickey, just exactly what do you mean by *like this*?"

In the darkness, thunder and lightning flashed in her eyes. With her hot Irish temper flaring, she answered tersely, "I … don't … want … it … to … be … like … this …" She continued a little calmer. "On prom night you'll need a reservation to get in here. No matter how you'll explain staying out all night, no one really believes that you didn't lose your virginity. I just don't want us to do it here or in some sleazy motel." Then becoming more adamant, she exclaimed, "And I don't want it to be on the night of the prom." Finally she was silent.

Sam's mind was full of questions he knew there were no answers for and answers he had no questions for. He was totally confused and didn't say a word. Afraid that he would reignite the storm, he started the car and drove to safety—home. They parked in the back of the house near the garage. Both of them sat in the darkness, not uttering a word. Sam gently folded Mickey in his arms and kissed her lovingly for a few moments. When they finally came up for air, he softly suggested, "Let's get some rest tonight. We'll discuss this tomorrow."

There was no immediate response from Mickey. She just stared at him with a devilish smile on her face. "There's no tomorrow. There's just tonight," she said. "Everyone's asleep, so why wait for tomorrow?"

They got out of the car, closing the doors quietly and made their way up to the hideaway. As they groped their way through the darkness to the back room, Sam realized that this was not one of her spur-of-the-moment fantasies. This little Irish she-devil had orchestrated the entire scenario. There were two bell-shaped, red glass candle lamps that he had never seen before. Like a magician she also produced a bottle of wine. Mickey lit the candles, and the room was bathed in a warm red glow. Her red hair seemed to radiate in the semidarkness. Sam opened the wine and poured two glasses full. They linked arms as she drank from his glass and he drank from hers. When the glasses were empty, they set them softly on the table.

Holding his hand, she led him to the bed. Mickey sat down and gently pulled Sam down next to her. She unbuttoned her blouse and leaned back slightly so it slipped off her shoulders. She turned her back completely to him, moving ever closer. "You can do the honors," she whispered. He undid her bra and lovingly cupped her breasts. They were full and firm. Sam could feel her nipples harden as he caressed them between his fingers. She gasped with pleasure, and he held her close to him for a long while. Slowly he undressed her, admiring her tiny waist and long, slim legs. She stood before him like a goddess. He started to disrobe, but she interrupted him. "No, Sam, let me undress you," she implored. Her fingers unbuttoned his shirt and caressed his smooth chest. Ripples of desire shot through his muscular body. He quickly helped her remove the rest of his garments.

The lovers passionately explored each other's bodies. She felt like warm velvet in his arms. He could wait no longer. He entered her body slowly. He couldn't bear to hurt her. She shuddered at first and then rose to meet his thrusts. It felt as though their minds were on fire with passion. Their very souls connected, floating on a cloud of ecstasy. The two became one, alone in the universe, surrounded only by the force of their love.

Sam and Mickey did make love on prom night. It didn't bother her at all. When he asked about her virginity, she jokingly replied, "I've already given."

CHAPTER 12

Race day for the Marshall Whitney Cup dawned cool and dry. Unfortunately, by the time they were ready to start, clouds had come rolling in. A light drizzle made the course slippery. There were twenty-six cars in the race as the starting signal was given. Sam was in twelfth position, buried in the middle of the pack. The roar of all the engines accelerating simultaneously sent chills up his spine. His adrenaline was really flowing.

Harmon Gunther, Glen Stewart, and Ron Nelson were the quickest off the line. When the first lap ended, Larry Watkins, Doug Hackett, Ben Sava, and Bruce Gatney were closing in on them. These drivers were followed by Andy Fitzpatrick, Rudy Michaels, Scott Wilson, and Sam. Bringing up the rear were Carl Patterson and Dan Razzado. They had a quarter of a lap lead on the rest of the mob. Buried somewhere back in the crowd were Sam's teammates, Jerry Burke and Larry Bogart.

Coming around the second lap, there was some heavy bumping and sliding. A few of the cars were fishtailing as they raced toward the far turn. One of them was Rudy Michaels. The rain had started coming down a little heavier, and the car in front of Rudy was completely swamped with water from the wet track. This waterfall blurred the driver's vision, and he careened off the railing hitting the car alongside of him. Unable to regain control of his car, Rudy rammed into the guardrail head on. The momentum of the crash forced the car under the rail and decapitated Rudy. No one realized what had happened. The heavy rain had cut their visibility in half. Cars were rebounding off each other all around the track.

Jerry Burke's steering wheel came off in his hand, causing him to also lose control. Larry Bogart, who was driving next to him, tried swerving to avoid a collision, but it was too late. Both cars collided and became fused together. Completely out of control, they made a sharp right turn as though they were observing a detour sign. They crashed through the fence, became airborne, and landed on top of a row of parked cars. Miraculously, both drivers escaped serious injury and jumped out of their cars seconds before they exploded.

As they watched the massive heap erupt into a great ball of flames, Larry exclaimed, "Wow! That was one hell of a flight!"

Jerry quickly replied, "Yeah! Remind me never to fly that airline again."

As the race continued, coming around the far turn in the tenth lap, Sam managed to push the Blazer into fourth position. Harmon Gunther and Glen Stewart, who were leading the first six laps, began falling back. Gunther had pulled off somewhere between the seventh and eighth laps with his rear end smoking. Stewart hit an oil slick coming out of the turn during the ninth lap. Losing control, he sideswiped Ron Nelson. Their wheels locked, and they were unable to break free. Coming out of the straightaway, both cars couldn't make the turn. They barreled through the guardrail together, becoming airborne, and flew over the embankment. The two cars rolled over each other and landed upside down. Then they burst into flames.

During the thirteenth lap, Sam's right front wheel started to shimmy. He tried to hold the Blazer steady to finish, but it wouldn't respond. He had to pull in for a pit stop. Mickey and Tom had some choice words for Sam. They were angry because he hadn't come in immediately when the wheel initially went bad. Tom got to work and deftly changed the tire while Sam remained seated in the car. Mickey was able to hand Tom a wrench when she stopped in midair.

"Sam, my God! Your eyes!" she shouted. She threw the wrench over to Tom and ran for the first aid kit. Returning in a few seconds, she pushed his head back over the rear support and put some drops in his eyes. "How did your eyes get so inflamed?" she asked.

Sam explained, "The rain caused moisture to build up inside my goggles. Every time I lifted them and placed them on my forehead to clear, the rain pelted my eyes."

As the eye drops settled in, she pushed Sam's head forward again and taped the top of his helmet. "Keep your goggles on. I sprayed them. They shouldn't fog up again."

Tom had already replaced the tire and adjusted the wheel. He put the cap back on the fuel tank after filling it up. Sam started to pull away, but Tom stopped him for a second. "Give yourself some room. Those guys are crazy out there."

Sam shot back onto the track more than a little disturbed by Tom's deep concern for his safety. He wondered if it had something to do with those disastrous accidents in the earlier laps. Maybe those guys didn't survive. Sam reproached himself for not remembering to ask. *It's probably better that I didn't*, he thought.

Once back on the track, Sam found himself in a logjam of cars. He stayed with the pack through the fourteenth and fifteenth laps. He was still trying to find an opening in the sixteenth lap when the car in front of him lost its left rear wheel. The wheel just disintegrated. The car spun around hitting two cars to the right of him and crashed into someone coming from behind. The car slammed into the iron rail and split apart as it burst into flames. Everyone else seemed to regain control. Suddenly Sam found himself in the pen. He floored the accelerator and started to widen the gap between him and the rest of the pack.

During the nineteenth lap, Sam started closing in on the leaders with Sava out in front, Watkins a few lengths behind, and Hackett and Gatney fighting for third place. Andy Fitzpatrick and Scott Wilson had exchanged fourth and fifth positions as they were going around the far turn. Coming into the straightaway, Watkins developed an oil leak, spilling over the track behind him. The oil slick sent Hackett and Gatney into a spin. Both cars bounced off each other as they spun wildly. Locking wheels, they barrel-rolled through the air a few times and eventually crashed through the fence, hitting a reserve fuel tank and exploding. The explosion sent a fiery stream of flames into the grandstand, and people scrambled for safety. Watkins headed for the pit, leaving a trail of black smoke, and burst into flames as he pulled in.

Going into the twentieth lap, Sam was in fourth place behind Sava, Fitzpatrick, and Wilson. He felt that he could pick up some distance coming out of the next turn when suddenly he was bumped from behind. He tried to look back but couldn't turn far enough around to see who had hit him. Then another car pulled up on his left. Sam thought he was trying to pass and couldn't understand why the other car was so close. The track was wide open on his side. Then the other driver slowed down, falling behind slightly, until his front wheel was parallel with Sam's back wheel. Trying to make it look like he was having difficulty passing Sam, he accelerated and rammed the back wheel, making it seem as though it was done accidentally.

The jarring caused Sam's head to whip from side to side. He felt something snap in the back of his neck, accompanied by a sharp pain that traveled between his shoulders and down his spine. Unable to turn his head without severe pain, Sam had to pull in. As he came to a stop, Mickey and Tom came running toward him.

With clenched fists, they both yelled, "What the hell was going on out there?"

"I don't know," Sam replied.

Mickey asked, "Sam, did you cut them off or bump them or something?"

He answered, "I didn't even notice them in the race. They must have been lying back in the pack waiting for me to get into the open."

Mickey looked at the entry list and yelled, "Number forty is Carl Patterson and number forty-nine is Dan Razzado. Do you know these guys? Are the names familiar?"

Sam shouted back, "I never heard of them."

The pain in his neck seemed to be getting worse, and his vision was blurred. Mickey and Tom could see that he was hurt badly. Tom helped him out if the car and asked for Sam's goggles. "What for?" Sam questioned.

Tom stiffened his jaw, and in a hard, determined voice, said, "I want the Blazer to finish the race. I'm not gonna let those bastards stop us!"

Grabbing the gobbles out of Sam's hands, Tom jumped into the car and sped off. He thundered back onto the track and pushed the

Blazer at full throttle. By the twenty-eighth lap, he had made up the lost time.

Sam remembered telling Mickey, "If Tom keeps pushing the Blazer to the limit the way he was, she'll blow up."

It certainly had enough power to outperform any of the cars in the race. However, the driver had to ease off once in a while to let her cool down and catch her breath. They flagged down Tom twice, but he apparently chose to ignore the signal.

Tom was coming up to the leaders with his foot to the floor. As he closed in fast, the only thing that stood between him and the front line was one of the guys who bumped Sam, Dan Razzado. Tom had to get around him. He challenged Razzado to the right, but Razzado cut him off. Tom knew he would have to catch Razzado off guard. He pulled back, making Razzado believe that he was coming from the right again. Razzado thought Tom was bluffing. He would be foolish to try to repeat the same maneuver. Razzado held his position. Tom accelerated, faking a pass on the right. Razzado moved far right to cut him off. Tom hit the brake for a split second and cut sharply to the left. Razzado adjusted what he thought was just enough, but Tom went wide and Razzado couldn't stop him. For that instant, he was open to pass. The Blazer would have to give him all the power she had. Tom pushed the accelerator to the floor with all the strength he could muster. The car engine roared louder than it had ever roared before. Blazer #1 started pulling away.

The crowd of forty thousand strong was going wild. They had never seen an exhibition of determination like this before. They knew that if Blazer #1 got past #49, it could catch up to the leaders and pass them too. In a last-ditch effort, just as Tom had almost passed Razzado before, Razzado purposely swerved his car sharply to the left, hitting Tom broadside. The impact jarred both drivers. Razzado, shaken momentarily, released his pressure on the accelerator, slowing him down. As the car pulled back, tragedy struck. His left front wheel caught the right back wheel of the Blazer. Hooked together, both cars went into a furious spin and careened off the track. Cartwheeling wildly, they somersaulted over the guardrail, landed in a grassy field, and exploded. Tom, trapped in the car, died on impact. Razzado was thrown free but died of internal injuries a week later without ever gaining consciousness.

Sam always believed that they were out to get him. They didn't see Tom and him switch places. Razzado obviously thought Sam was still driving, and Tom died in his place. Sam could never have proved what he believed. Carl Paterson, the driver of car #42 disappeared, and Razzado was dead. There was gossip that filtered back to Mickey and Sam before the race that "there was no way a Jap would win this race." They had just kissed each other and shrugged it off. Now Tom was dead, and Sam would always feel responsible for his death.

CHAPTER 13

SARAH, SAM'S SISTER, REMAINED after school to work out in the pool with the rest of the swimming team. They had a meet coming up in a few days. The team wanted to make sure their timing was synchronized. The one-hundred-meter freestyle belonged to her, and she had all the trophies to prove it. Now the coach wanted her to anchor the four-hundred-meter relay. Sarah's legs were muscular and powerful. After years of training, she could kick like a dynamo.

Stanley Brown, her steady beau, had seen her earlier in the day. Sarah had told him about her plan to stay after school to practice with the team. He said, "I'll hang around and drive you home. Maybe we'll stop for a soda later." She liked that idea. Besides, Stan wouldn't mind watching all the girls bouncing around in their tight bathing suits.

When the workout was over, the girls went back to the locker room for showers. They were laughing and joking. Funny little quips about how each had performed echoed through the building. Some of the larger, more endowed girls complained that the coach spent more time staring at their breasts than correcting their swimming techniques. They finished dressing and said good night.

Stan was waiting at the locker room door as Sarah came out. He held her hand, and they walked over to his parked car. They sat there for a while looking at each other in the semidarkness. The parking lot light cast a warm glow across her face. Her hair, still a little wet, draped down over her shoulders. She leaned back, rested her head on his arm, and said, "Please excuse the way I look, Stan."

"Silly," he replied. "I think you're beautiful." He kissed her and looked adoringly into her brown eyes.

She softly brushed the hair off his face. "I thought you were taking me for a soda."

"Are you kidding?" he queried. "I wait for you all day and half the night and all I get is one kiss."

She gently placed her fingers on his lips and requested again, "Soda, please."

Stan smiled and asked her, "Do you know how much I love you?"

Sara, nodding her head, persisted, "Yes, soda."

At the swimming meet, the team as a whole was outstanding. Sarah won the one-hundred-meter freestyle and outdid her hottest rival to win the two-hundred-meter as well. By the time the relay portion of the contest came up, she was exhausted. She had stretched out on a bench and Stan, who always accompanied her for moral support, was massaging her shoulders. The whistle blew signaling the teams to take their positions at the edge of the pool. Sarah looked out of place as she stood behind her teammates. They were all five or six inches taller than she was. To see the start of the race, she had to lean sideways.

The first two girls on her team managed to keep up with the leaders. As Sarah's third teammate dove in, she hit the water hard. This caused her to lose a few strokes. By the time she touched the other end of the pool and returned, she was two-and-a-half body lengths behind the leader.

Sarah was in the ready position when her teammate completed her laps. Her strong hips propelled her through the air as though she was shot out of a cannon. When the leader approached the far side of the pool, Sarah had almost caught up with her. On the underwater turn, they both did well. As they surfaced, both girls were almost even. Sensing that she had almost overtaken the leader, Sarah turned on the steam. As she went for the finish, her arms felt heavy and tired, but her strong legs were kicking like high-speed pistons. The coach was right. He knew that she had the kick to win the relay. The team won the trophy, and Sarah got a special award for swimming the last lap in record-breaking time.

This time Stan was not alone as he waited for Sarah at the locker room door. A crowd of friends and parents, including Mr. and Mrs. Sagarra, had joined him. Behind the closed doors, they could hear the team screaming with joy. Then, without warning, the locker room door exploded open and they all came running out together. Sarah threw her arms around Stan's neck and held on lightly as he put his arms around her waist. He lifted her easily off the ground and spun her around and around until he almost collapsed from dizziness. Before he put her down, he kissed her. When she opened her eyes, there were her parents standing a few feet away, waiting patiently to congratulate their daughter. Sarah, slightly embarrassed and blushing, regained her composure. Taking Stan by the hand, she walked toward her father and mother.

Stan was concerned. He had met Sarah's parents before, but he hadn't learned enough about Japanese customs. There was no way to tell how they would react to such an exuberant display of emotion. He and Sarah stood face-to-face with them. Visions of a sacrificial lamb appeared in his mind. He was greatly relieved when Sarah's parents smiled and joyously congratulated her. Then her father turned his head and, seemingly as an afterthought, said, "Oh, hello, Stanley." With a twinkle in his eye and a large grin, Father was playfully chiding him.

As Sarah asked to be excused, Mother reminded them not to stay out too late. As the happy couple ran off, she yelled to them, "Where are you going?" Sarah looked back and said, "Just to Jaffy's Soda Shoppe. Stan's taking me for a soda."

Stan looked at her curiously. "You just spent the whole day in the water. How on earth can you be thirsty?"

When they got to Jaffy's, most of the team was already there whooping it up. Jaffy's was a popular meeting place where the local kids congregated. They danced to the blaring jukebox and screamed to each other over the loud music. With all the excitement, no one noticed the three strangers sitting in a side booth.

They weren't from the area. These guys had heard of Jaffy's and thought it would be a good place to pick up some girls.

One of the strangers was Mark Anderson. He was a heavy, muscular, and slovenly looking guy; his friends called him Marko. He was becoming agitated by all the attention Sarah was getting. Turning to his companions he said, "I can't believe they're praising that Japanese bitch." He made an obscene gesture. "We should show them how she really should be treated. C'mon, let's go." All three got up and walked out. Outside Marko said, "I've got a plan. We'll wait across the street in the car. When they leave, we'll follow them."

By the time the celebration ended, it was already dark outside. As the kids said good night and left, no one saw the three dark silhouettes in the car across the street. Stan and Sarah drove off and didn't notice that the strangers were following close behind. They drove a few blocks and stopped for a red light. Marko yelled, "This is our chance. Pull in front of 'em and put on the brakes. John, you stay in the car. Pete and me will go out and grab 'em."

It all happened so quickly that Stan and Sarah were taken completely by surprise. Marko pulled the door open and grabbled Sarah's arm. He dragged her out of the car, putting his hand over her mouth to muffle her screams. He picked her up and carried her to the waiting car. He was about to throw her into the back seat when he checked on Pete. Pete was having a tough time with Stan. Marko would have to go back and help him, but first he had to subdue Sarah. He hit her in the back of her neck momentarily paralyzing her. When she became limp in his arms, he threw her in the car.

Then he ran back to the other car and pushed Pete aside. "Let me get him," he snarled. Marko grabbed Stan's arm and brutally twisted it behind his back. Stan heard the bone snap and excruciating pain ran up his arm to his shoulder. Marko put his right hand over Stan's mouth, and he and Pete dragged him to the waiting car. They pushed him in on top of Sarah. Pete slammed the door shut and jumped into the front seat next to Marko. As Marko floored the accelerator, the squeal of the tires and the smell of burnt rubber filled the air as the car sped away.

Stan felt as if both of his arms were broken. He couldn't move either one. As he lay there on top of Sarah, he could feel her breathing. A feeling of extreme helplessness came over him as wild thoughts flooded his mind. When the car stopped, Marko said, "This spot's perfect." Stan felt himself being propped up on the backseat. Unable to move, he watched, stunned, as Marko and Pete removed Sarah's clothing. She regained consciousness and started to struggle. Still groggy and weak, it was easy for Marko to restrain her. He told Pete to get into the front seat.

He positioned Sarah's naked body partially upright and threw her over the top of the seat on her stomach with her head in the front seat and her buttocks facing him. Pete grabbed her hands and held her down.

Looking behind Marko at Stan, Pete asked, "What about him?"

Marko replied, "Let him watch. I'll show him what she's good for."

Marko unbuckled his belt and pulled his pants down. Then he spread her legs apart and savagely entered her from behind. Stan could hear Sarah make a feeble attempt to scream. The pain was more than she could bear and mercifully she fainted. When Marko was through violating her small, limp body, he fell back toward Stan. Though he couldn't see Marko's face, Stan knew that he was sweating profusely because of the strong foul odor. Marko turned to Stan and put his hand around his throat. "See, that's what she's good for," he snarled.

Leaning over Stan to open the door, Marko's fingers became entangled in the chain Stan was wearing. As he shoved him out, it ripped off and dangled from his hand. He held it closer to get a better look.

Marko yelled out, "This bastard's a Jew."

Pete replied, "How lucky can ya get? We got us a Jap and a Jew on the same night."

Pushing Sarah out the door, they drove off. In a state of semi-consciousness and reeling in pain, Stan crawled over to Sarah's side. Unable to move his arms, he rolled over on top of her to shield her bloody, naked body with his own. They were found that way in the morning, barely alive.

Mother's frantic calls all evening to the police had put them on alert. They immediately confirmed that the two brutalized victims were the teenagers they had been searching for. Mother arrived at the hospital moments after Sarah and Stan were brought in. When Mother was finally allowed to see Sarah, she was horrified and went into a state of shock. The rest of the family arrived shortly after. Sarah and Stan were still in the operating room. Everyone stayed close to Mother and tried to comfort her.

When word came that Sarah and Stan were being taken to their rooms, they all went up to see Sarah first. They were only there for a few minutes when Charlie abruptly turned around and started to leave.

Sam asked, "Charlie, where are you going?"

He replied, "I'll be right back."

He entered the men's ward, and the nurse guided him to Stan's private room. Charlie saw Stan propped up by what seemed to be a large pillow. His eyes were closed as if he were asleep. Stan's right arm was in a plaster cast. All the fingers in his left hand had been broken and were individually set. There was tape wrapped around his forehead that came down both sides of his face and ended under his chin. He looked as if he was wearing a blood-soaked white football helmet.

Charlie walked slowly and quietly toward the bed. Stan suddenly opened his eyes and quivered slightly as though frightened. The movement made his eyes cringe as pain shot through his body. Charlie just stared at him for a while. Then he said, "You look like you fell into a meat grinder. Did you recognize any of them, Stan?"

Stan hesitated for a few moments and answered, "No, but the guy who put his hand over my mouth had a tattoo of a devil's head in between his thumb and forefinger."

"How many of them were there?" Charlie queried.

"Three," answered Stan.

"Did they all rape her?" Charlie's voice was full of venom.

"No," answered Stan. "Only the guy with the tattoo. The other two held her until she passed out. The guy with the tattoo was so rough with her. They thought she was dead. They thought we were both dead."

Charlie touched Stan's shoulder gently and said, "Don't say anything about this conversation to anyone."

He started walking toward the door when Stan called out to him. "Charlie, what are you going to do?"

Charlie looked back with a revengeful sneer on his face. "You'll find out when you open your mail in a few days."

When Charlie entered Sarah's room, she was still in a coma. Mother was sitting at Sarah's bedside and holding her hand. Billy and Sam were standing by the window, silently staring into space. Father sat in a small chair next to them. His anguished voice kept asking, "Why? Why would anyone want to do this? How could they hurt her so badly?"

Charlie just stood there for a few minutes, not saying anything. Then he suddenly turned around and headed for the door. Sam ran across the room and grabbed his arm. He could feel the tension in his brother's muscles. Sam had to tighten his grip to keep Charlie from pulling away.

"Where are you going?" he asked.

"I have something to do," Charlie answered.

Sam could see that his eyes were full of tears. He pleaded with him, "Let the police handle it."

Charlie snapped back at him, "Oh yeah, how serious do you think a raped Jap and a beat-up Jew will be to them?" He pulled away from Sam and ran out.

CHAPTER 14

Charlie had a lot of close friends. Any one of them would have been more than willing to help him. Most of them had grown up together. They knew his family and had special feelings for Sarah. He confidentially spread the word that he was looking for a guy with a tattoo of a devil's head between his thumb and forefinger. Within a few days, Chuck Wagner, one of Charlie's former teammates, spotted this guy in one of the local bars. He had the devil tattoo on his hand, and they called him Marko. That day there had been a loud discussion about Japan's deteriorating relationship with America. Marko cut everyone short and shut them up. He stood up and gave his biased, racist version of the only thing he thought Japs were good for. Then he walked out. After asking around, Chuck found out that the loudmouth's full name was Mark Anderson. He was also able to find out where Marko lived.

Charlie thanked everyone for offering to help him, but he didn't want any of his friends to get into trouble. What he needed were people who could do the job and then disappear. They would have to be people he could trust. Charlie remembered a dance he had attended a few months back on the south end of town. He had been introduced to a group of Japanese radicals. These fanatics all had a common cause: They weren't going to allow themselves to be victimized anymore. If they were pushed, they vowed to push back—*hard!* Charlie contacted them. The young radicals responded as though they had been waiting for his call. Everyone had heard about Sarah, and this would be their chance to strike back.

The next day, Charlie and three of his newly acquired Japanese radicals were in a panel truck parked across the street from Marko's house. Now all they had to do was wait.

Charlie asked one of the guys, "Where did you get the truck?"

He replied, "We stole it from the cannery so we can dump it in the river when we're finished using it."

They had been in the truck for about two hours and darkness was setting in. Charlie was concerned about getting the wrong guy. Suddenly a car pulled up in front of the house and parked at the curb. There were three occupants who were passing a bottle around, each taking a swig before passing it on.

"Okay, Charlie, it's your move," one of his cohorts said. "But what if he's not the right guy?"

Charlie answered, "What's the difference? They're not Japanese. Let's kick the shit out of them anyway. I didn't steal this truck for nothing. Let's do this."

They started the motor and drove across the street, pulling up very close to the parked car and blocking the driver's side. No one was going to get out that way. Charlie and two others jumped out of the truck from the back doors with tire irons in their hands. They quickly ran around to the passenger side of the car and pulled the doors open.

The guy in the front seat put his hand on the roof of the car to pull himself upright. Charlie saw the devil's head tattoo. He hit Marko across the face with the tire iron. "He's the one," he yelled as he hit him again. Meanwhile, Charlie's comrades split the heads of the other two, not caring if they were or weren't Marko's accomplices. They did it just for fun. Besides, they figured that if the other two were friends with a bastard like Marko, they deserved everything they got.

Charlie pulled a dazed and bloody Marko from the car. "This one is coming with us," he said.

His helpers inquired, "What about his two friends?"

"Leave 'em," Charlie answered. "They're busted up enough, and besides, they're out cold. I'm sure they were too drunk to know what hit them."

They threw Marko into the back of the truck and drove off. After pulling into a dark, deserted parking lot, they stopped. Charlie put some adhesive tape across Marko's eyes as he started to regain consciousness and tried to get up. The other two pushed him back down so Charlie could tape his mouth.

Charlie sat back for a few seconds to catch his breath and gave Marko time to regain full consciousness. When he was wide awake, Charlie took a straight-edge barber's razor from his pocket. He flipped it open while the other two guys held Marko's hands and feet down. Charlie cut open Marko's shirt, exposing his chest. Then he straddled Marko's body and sat on his thighs. Charlie methodically shaved the hair off his chest. When he finished, he positioned the razor between his thumb and forefinger as he would ordinarily hold a pen. Cutting deep into Marko's hairless chest, Charlie wrote, "I raped Sarah Sagarra." The other two had to tighten their grip as Marko squirmed in excruciating pain.

Then Charlie took the razor and ran it down Marko's cheek, saying, "You know what we need now? A present for the Jew and you're gonna give it to him." Putting his hand under Marko's belt, he slit it open with the razor. Charlie slid down lower on Marko's legs so he could pull his pants down. Marko was shaking with fright, and they could hear his muffled screams and garbled pleading through the tape. Charlie reached out for Marko's penis. Holding it securely in his left hand, he said in a serious tone, "Lie very still. I don't want to take more than I need." Marko's body became stiff as the cold blade cut into his penis.

Suddenly Charlie yelled to one of his comrades, "Give me your shoelace."

"What for? Do you want to tie it into a bow?" he queried.

"No, a tourniquet," Charlie replied. "I slipped. The whole damn thing came off!"

Marko's body became limp as he went into shock and passed out.

"Charlie, you didn't cut the whole thing off? Did you?" they queried in unison.

Hesitating for a second, he replied, "No, but I should have. I only circumcised him. This little piece is for Stan. C'mon, let's get out of here and dump this pile of shit."

Charlie mailed the piece of skin he removed from Marko with a short note to Stan later that day.

The incident was never reported, and as planned, everyone involved disappeared, including Charlie. The war in Europe was in full swing, and Charlie decided to enlist in the army.

"There was so much hate in my heart that I had to get away," Charlie wrote home to his family. "Over here at least we know who the enemy is. They're right in front of us, on the other side of the line. I feel like an American defending my country and destroying our enemies. At home I felt as though *I* was the enemy."

Charlie became part of a combat unit mostly comprised of Japanese Americans. They all had one thing in common: they were fighting for their country—America—and they fought with bravery and valor. They continuously defeated elite, battle-hardened Nazi troops. They destroyed entire divisions as they relentlessly pushed forward. Charlie's unit became one of the most decorated battalions in the history of the United States Army.

CHAPTER 15

THE MONTHS FOLLOWING TOM'S funeral were difficult ones for all of them. All their friends felt the deep loss, especially Sam. He would always remember on the day before the race for the Marshall Whitney Cup, Tom had suggested that Sam should take the Blazer out for a spin since it was a one-driver race. He had justified his reason, "I have taken her across the finish line in the cross-country, and I want you to see what that feels like."

Sam had rejected the idea because Tom was the better driver. Tom had laughingly replied, "I'm only good in mud mixed with horse shit. This race is all on paved roads. It doesn't have the right ingredients for me, and I just wouldn't enjoy it." He had thrown the keys to Sam and said, "This one's all yours, pal."

They had been part of each other's lives for so many years. Sam would never forgive himself for letting Tom finish the race, throwing that final block for him, one that cost him his life.

Sam's relationship with Mickey started to change. The hours they used to spend holding each other and sharing their innermost thoughts became quite somber. She slowly began withdrawing. One evening as he held her in his arms, she suddenly started pulling away from him.

"Sam, I can't go on like this," she cried. Tears were rolling down her cheeks like tiny waterfalls. Trying desperately to hold back the tears, she slowly and somewhat pleadingly repeated herself. "I just can't go on like this anymore." Hesitating to gasp for a deep breath of air, she continued, "Every time I kiss you, I see all of us together—you, me, and Tom kidding around, laughing and joking with each other. Then suddenly my mind erupts. I keep seeing the car rolling over and over and the fiery explosion. It's horrible."

She buried her face in her hands while shaking her head. "I just can't take it anymore." She paused and slowly proceeded. "I need some time away. Mother suggested a college out west and I'm going to try it."

Sam's feelings were in turmoil. The memory of Tom's death haunted him also. Their friendship had been something quite special. Now, with Mickey going away, his brain felt as though it was short-circuiting. Everything was all mixed up, and Sam was hurting badly. His heart was heavy. He had lost two people he had loved for many years. A part of him had also died in that crash. All the plans and dreams that Mickey and he had made were cremated in the flames that caused Tom's death.

The month ahead became unbearable. Every time he looked at the clubhouse, Sam felt that he could hear the three of them joking and laughing inside. He slowly realized, like Mickey, that he had to get away—far away. He decided to enlist in the US Naval Air Force.

Sam was sent for training and afterward assigned to a naval air control unit on the island of Oahu in Hawaii. Flying was the therapy he needed, rekindling the flame in his mind for adventure. He was sent on routine control missions and loved them. Flying above the clouds, unable to see the earth below, made him feel as if he was in a different world, a better world whose horizon was just beyond the next cloud. Every time he went up, Sam would try to reach that horizon. It was always just beyond his reach, and he would have to come back to Earth.

For the first time in his life, he was surrounded by tens of thousands of Japanese. They were friendly and accepted him as one of their own. Amazingly, he began to think of himself as one of them, a unique and puzzling feeling—unique because here he was one of many, and puzzling because they were working side by side. The Japanese people were all over the bases. If they wanted to obtain confidential information, it was at their fingertips. If hostilities did break out, it was expected that they would be in the middle of it. They were just Japanese and Japanese Americans.

Meanwhile, three thousand miles away, the racist bigots found no distinction. They made us all the enemy—*all Japs!*

CHAPTER 16

By February 1941, CMI had started production on the first completed engine, forecast to come off the line by the end of the year. One evening Jim McBride and Robbie Kantor stayed late. There seemed to be a minor problem in the crankshaft assembly. They thought if they worked through the night, which was not an uncommon practice for them, they'd iron out the kinks and prevent shutting down production. It would be a tremendously needed psychological boost for all their supporters and their own morale if they could produce CM101 on schedule as predicted.

Terry Woodward offered to stay, but Jim told her, "It really isn't necessary. If we get these bugs out, you'll have enough to do in the morning, rewriting these specifications." To further intimidate her into going home, he picked up a stack of paper six inches thick and waved them at her.

She looked back at him and suggested, "At least let me go out and get you guys some sandwiches. I don't want to find you dead when I come back in the morning."

Robbie Kantor yelled out from the other side of the room, "That sounds great to me. I'm starving!"

Jim agreed, making her promise to leave immediately after supplying them with the impromptu dinner.

Jim and Robbie went right to work. They had a tough night ahead and wanted to get started. They were already taking apart the shaft assembly. Being alone, they had taken the precaution of making sure all the exterior exits were secured. When the doorbell rang, they weren't concerned. They knew it was Terry returning with their meal.

Robbie said, "I'll get the door. I could eat a horse."

As he opened the door, he could sense that something was wrong. Terry wasn't her usual jolly self and didn't walk right in. She just stood there for a moment holding a bag, which he assumed was the sandwiches. He asked kindly, "Aren't you coming in?"

Suddenly everything went crazy. She did come in but not on her own volition. She was viciously pushed from behind, almost shoving the bag down Robbie's throat. The unexpected force of her entry knocked him over backward. He fell down and his head hit the sharp edge of a desk, rendering him unconscious.

There were three men wearing Batman masks. One of them held Terry with his arm around her throat. With the other arm, the masked man twisted her arm behind her back, incapacitating her. Yelling across to Jim, he ordered, "Don't make any sudden moves! Stand perfectly still or I'll snap her neck! It would be a shame to see this pretty little bitch die so young."

Jim heeded the warning and didn't move. Standing perfectly still, the other two masked intruders immobilized him. Using a pair of handcuffs, they restrained his hands behind him and sat him down on a chair. With another set of cuffs, they secured his ankles. Then the leader, who was still holding Terry, yelled to one of his henchmen, "Check out the one on the floor."

The burly man bent over Robbie to check his pulse and said, "Boss, I think he's dead, but I'll cuff him anyway."

Still holding Terry, the leader ordered his accomplices to relieve him. As they grabbed her hands and feet, he said, "Before you cuff her, strip her!" As he glanced around the facility, he noticed two vats the size of bathtubs. One was filled with acid for cleaning tools. The other was full of a high-grade, amber-colored lubricating oil used on the engine's mechanical parts. During the assembly process, each vat had a chain pulley hanging above it to lift and support heavy objects for submersion.

Pointing to the vat filled with oil, the leader said, "Throw her in there and hang her up to dry!" Walking over to Jim, he stopped and said, "Now what are we going to do with you?" He put his hand on his chin as he contemplated. "I got it," he exclaimed. "You like the engine so much, we'll let you make love to one of them." He called out to his masked assistants, "Aren't you guys through with her?"

They had just finished submerging Terry, and she was completely covered with oil. They put the hook of the pulley around her handcuffs and hoisted her above the vat.

"I need you guys over here to give me a hand with this one," he said, pointing to Jim. "Take off his shirt."

All three dragged the shackled man over to a prototype of the CM101 engine that was used for testing. They lifted him up and prostrated him over the top of the engine on his stomach. The leader continued with his diabolical torture. "Okay, now tie his hands and feet together under the engine so he can't get off." Pointing to the start button, he told one of the guys to push it. The engine roared to a start. Jim's pain was agonizingly unbearable. The vibration of the engine made him feel as though he was being ripped apart. His skin was burning up from the heat that emanated from the motor. Grinding his teeth and cringing in pain, Jim required all the effort his brain could generate to not scream. He'd die before he gave them that satisfaction. When the leader of the group thought Jim had had enough, he ordered his associate to shut down the engine. Jim was semiconscious. He could barely understand what the assailants were saying. It was like being in a fog with someone trying to communicate with you from far off in the distance.

They started to leave, stopping momentarily by Terry as she hung over the vat with her feet still submerged in the oil. The leader placed his hand on her shoulder and said, "This is just a warning." He slid his hand down her oil-slicked body, stopping to fondle her breasts for a few seconds. "Tell your boss, he'd be smart if he sold out."

Still fondling Terry's stomach, he placed his other hand on her back. Then, with both hands moving in a circular motion, he began massaging her body, stopping long enough to comment on what a nice belly button she had. Then he slid both hands down around her thighs. As both of his hands met above her knees, he locked his fingers together so his hands were between her legs. Slowly he began sliding them back up, stopping at her crotch. He rotated them slightly until she opened her eyes. While the fingers of his left hand were skimming through her public hair, he remarked, "Tell your boss, if we have to come back here, we'll go all the way! Especially you and me, babe."

CHAPTER 17

SAM HAD ONLY BEEN away from home a few months when he received a letter from Mother telling him about the problems Father was having. As the anti-Japanese sentiment intensified, so did the threats. She also told him about the break-in at CMI and what they had done to Terry and his good friend Jim McBride. The letter left him devastated. Thinking he should go home to lend some moral support, he asked for special leave but was turned down. The reasons, they said, were due to intensified movements by the Japanese in the Pacific and that he was needed for special assignment.

The decoding department desperately needed someone who understood Japanese and could speak it fluently. Sam joined a group of some pretty sharp guys. They had already deciphered a very small portion of the gibberish the Japanese were sending over the air. Sam's job was to see if they were garbling the messages deliberately to create confusion. From the information they were able to put together, they felt sure the Japanese were going to mobilize their forces soon. They just weren't sure where. The base was put on daily alerts. On December 5,

1941, orders circulated stating that communications with the mainland would be limited to specifically designated official personnel.

On December 7th, a thunderous explosion awakened Sam. Startled, he sat up in his cot. There was a second larger explosion. The force of the blast sandwiched him in the bedding like a hot dog and blew him out the window. Dazed, he managed to roll under the crawl space of the barracks with the cot mattress over his head. He lay there as the inferno from hell was being unleashed all around him. A bomb hit a row of planes loaded with fuel right in front of him. The building he was under blew up with a fiery intensity that lifted it off its foundation, and the heat set his mattress on fire.

Instinctively jumping to his feet, Sam looked like a human fireball as he ran panic stricken with the flaming mattress still wrapped around him. Fortunately, he hadn't gone more than a few steps when he was doused by the cooling sprays of extinguishers. His fire-fighting buddies were all over him in seconds.

"Why did you drag that burning mattress with you?" one of the guys asked.

Sam replied, "I didn't realize I was still holding it."

He owed them his life. He didn't realize it then, but they would pass that debt back and forth many times. It took a few days before they knew the extent of the terrible death toll. Sam was one of the lucky ones, escaping with only superficial burns.

CHAPTER 18

The break-in at the plant left Father extremely disturbed. Although he was bitter and disillusioned, what bothered him most was the cruel treatment his employees had suffered. He was deeply hurt. Father was an honorable man and accepted everyone who worked with him as family. He never used the expression "worked for him."

When everyone was well enough, he called a meeting. Speaking in a low emotional voice, he said, "We have come a long way together. We have endured hardships and many disappointments, but we have succeeded in creating something that no one expected. Our engine, the CM101, is far superior and will outperform anything our competitors have on the drawing board for years to come. Now they won't let us produce it. They won't let us keep it. Furthermore, if I don't agree to sell out, I will be put out!" He hesitated momentarily for a drink of water.

Jim McBride, still in pain with every deep breath he took, interrupted his address. "Excuse me, sir. If it's our safety you're concerned about, I think I can speak for Terry, Robbie, and everyone else here. You brought us together and made us a team. This plant has become our second home. We've experienced many letdowns and literally survived an attack of barbarians. Our tenacity alone kept us going. Now we have another test. If we let these people intimidate us, everything we have worked for all these years will be gone. I, for one, have a personal vengeance to satisfy. Now I have to speak for myself. You have been the father I never had. You supported every crazy idea that I ever dreamed up. The faith you had in all of us is the reason CM101 became a reality. I could never turn my back on you!"

Everyone quietly nodded their heads in total agreement. Terry was crying softly.

Father had nothing to say. He couldn't if he wanted to. The emotional outburst had floored him. With tears in his eyes, he leaned back in his chair, turned his palms up, and shrugged his shoulders. Somehow he managed a choked reply. "Okay, we'll continue."

The dedicated group quickly got their act together. Inside of two weeks, they had the plant rolling again. With a few minor adjustments, they were back on schedule, more determined than ever to complete their first production of engine CM101 by year's end. The next few months passed without any incidents, except for the threatening phone calls. They continued with one difference. Obscenity was added.

The end of the year was only three weeks away. CMI made plans for a big party. Celebrating the incoming new year, they planned on christening the first engine off the line with a bottle of champagne. There was another little ceremony the group was planning. Terry, Jim, and Rob had a jeweler make a model of the CM101. It had been ordered months earlier. The charm was engraved with something special and the original production delivery date. In a place where superstition abounded, everyone agreed not to change it. They decided that they all would give it to Father together. When they went to his office, the door was open and the radio was on. Father was sitting slouched over his desk with his head in his hands. He looked up as they entered.

Terry, holding the present, asked, "Are you all right, sir?"

He raised his head and slowly looked at them as if they were strangers. "Japan has attacked Pearl Harbor," he solemnly announced.

They stood there in shock for what seemed to be an eternity. Before anyone spoke, Terry finally walked to the desk and placed the present before him. Softly she said, "This is for you, Mr. Sagarra. I'm sorry." Hesitating, she asked, "What will happen now?"

He replied, "The worst has already happened! Only God knows how it will end." Regaining his composure, he reached out for the package, politely saying, "Thank you all for your faith in me, but I'm afraid the road ahead has become buried in heavy fog."

As he unwrapped the miniature gold engine, it glistened in his hand. He forced a gentle smile and said, "Very appropriate." He turned it toward them and stretched his hand across the desk so they could read the inscription.

Terry read it out loud: "To Kei Sagarra—a man with a dream." Her voice became inaudible as she read the date, "December 7, 1941."

With nothing left to say, they went back to work.

A few weeks later, on Dec. 30, 1941, one day before the New Year, the phone rang after Father had gone to bed. He answered it and the caller told him, "CMI is burning just like we promised it would." Father fumbled with the phone, his fingers shaking uncontrollably. Mother felt him trembling and asked, "Kei, what is it?"

He passed the phone to her in disgust. Jumping out of bed and dressing quickly, he yelled back to her, "Call Jim McBride and Rob

Kantor." As he ran out the door, he concluded, "Tell them CMI is on fire."

By the time Father, Jim, and Rob arrived at the plant, the fire had engulfed the entire building. When it reached the gasoline tanks, there was an fiery, earth-shattering explosion that lit up the sky for miles. The three men just stood there. With tears rolling down their cheeks, they watched the destruction helplessly. CMI was gone.

CHAPTER 19

JAPAN HAD STRUCK! SUDDENLY the United States was at war and on its knees! The communication blackout to the mainland expanded now to include everyone except headquarters and commanding officers. Sam was becoming frustrated and bored with his daily routine. Sitting in the decoding room desperately trying to unscramble that nonsensical gibberish was starting to drive him crazy.

Holding out as long as he could, he finally approached his commanding officer, Harlin (Harley) Cooper. Commander Cooper was a tall, square-shouldered, lean and mean Texan, who used to have a strong accent. He said he lost it "yellin' at sons a bitches!" To emphasize his toughness, he'd say, "I wasn't soaked in oil. I grew up pushin' a mule and workin' the farm." Sam explained his frustrations and pleaded to be sent into action.

Looking at him puzzled, Commander Cooper said, "Sagarra, the Japanese are sinking our ships like crazy. Hardly a day goes by that one don't go down. Why would anyone in his right mind want to go out there?"

Sam replied, "Sir, it seems as though all my life I've been taking"—his mind rushed back through time thinking of the guys on the football team trying to protect him, Tom losing his life for him, and Mickey unconditionally giving him her love—"and taking. I have a desperate need to give something back, sir, even if it's my life."

Still not giving in, Commander Cooper tried reasoning with Sam again. Becoming more personal, he said, "Look, Sam, whether you realize it or not, you're not just a piece of furniture around here. You're one of our secret weapons. You are! Right now, at this moment, you're our most valuable asset. The only way we can regain control of this situation is by the element of surprise. Our ships and planes are out there, what's left of 'em. We have to buy some time. You find out where the enemy is going to attack next. Then our ships will concentrate on getting there first and prepare one hell of a welcoming party! That's your job, Sam." Hesitating, almost as an after-thought, he said, "Thousands of American lives will be depending on you."

As Commander Cooper turned and walked out of the room, Sam just stood there for a few minutes. Cooper's words still echoed in his mind. "Thousands of American lives are depending on you."

In the following weeks, tension rose to a boiling point. They were reasonably sure the enemy knew that the Americans had broken their code. Not having time to change it, they just quadrupled the amount of messages sent, adding some extra gibberish to confuse them all the more. However, there was something that the decoders had picked up that was being repeated in a familiar sequence. After a few days of intensive deduction, they were pretty sure where the next strike would be. To say that they broke the entire code would be a gross overstatement. They understood one word out of every ten or fifteen intercepted. This accomplishment did not give them the ability to put together a message that they could say was cast in stone. However, it would be formidable enough to sink the fleet if they were wrong.

The information was passed on to headquarters. Based on their "shooting craps" predictions, headquarters would have to make the final decision—whether or not to commit their crippled fleet to a decisive battle that could lose the war for America. If they were wrong, the dice would be in Japan's corner. As luck would have it, Sam did get another chance to fly. The commanders believed that their prediction was correct. However, if the Japanese were going to launch an attack, they would be counting heavily on the element of surprise. If the enemy fleet was getting close, they would maintain radio silence. Headquarters needed someone to fly a reconnaissance plane as far out as possible. The mission would be to try to pick up some slight signal, even an unidentifiable bleep or blurp, to reassure headquarters that they had made the right decision. Sam was chosen for the job.

His copilot was a Texan, Dean Jasper, who was well over six feet tall and probably just as wide. Sam didn't think he would fit into the cockpit. Dean spoke with a long Texas drawl, greeting Sam as they met at the plane. "Hi, Saagaarra. Ya flyin' with me taday?"

Sam replied, "Ya, I'm flyin' with ya taday."

They got in and took off.

For the first hour or so, Dean rambled on, describing his hometown in Texas. Flying above the clouds, they were approximately three hundred miles out when Dean finally asked, "Hey, Saagaarra, what the hell are ya lookin' for?"

Sam replied, "The enemy."

Dean asked inquisitively, "What the hell do they look like?"

Sam wanted to say, "Turn around, you dummy." However, he thought better of it. He knew that Dean was referring to ships. They were out as far as they could go without running out of fuel. With nothing to report, they returned to the base. Nevertheless, four days later, the enemy proved them correct.

The Japanese advanced toward the predicted target, and the American fleet was waiting strategically positioned. This time, the element of surprise was on the American side. After a week of intensive bombardment, the battle turned in America's favor. Most of the Japanese fleet was demolished, and the remaining ships were crippled. They had dealt a devastating blow to the enemy's offensive, and the conflict became a turning point in the war. America needed this one to bolster their shattered morale, and they got it!

With the enemy suppressed, the communications blackout was lifted. Sam had not heard from his family in over six and a half months. He had tried calling home, but the operator told him that the number was no longer in service. He thought that they had it changed or removed due to the threatening, obscene calls. Sam's concern heightened when his letters returned unanswered. He requested leave, which was granted. The trip home took a few days. He was full of excitement and anticipation at the thought of seeing his family after the long separation.

CHAPTER 20

When he finally arrived home, Sam could see immediately that something was amiss. The shrubs were growing wildly. The grass, along with the weeds, was about two feet high. Father loved his plants. He would never let them become that overgrown and messy if he could help it. When Sam tried the front door, it was locked. Not having a key, he went next door to the McGoverns. He was a little apprehensive because he hadn't seen them for such a long time. What would they tell him about his parents? What would he do if Mickey answered the door? Finally, getting up enough nerve, he rang the bell. It felt like an eternity before Mrs. McGovern answered the door. She was definitely surprised to see him.

"Sam, oh my God. I can't believe it's you. Come on in," she said. Taking his hand, she led him into the living room where Jack McGovern was reading a newspaper in his favorite chair. She joyfully said, "Jack, look who's here! It's Sam, Sam Sagarra."

McGovern, astonished at the appearance of Sam standing before him, exclaimed, "My God, son, we thought you were dead. It's been so long without any word from you."

Sam explained about the communications blackout and all his futile attempts to contact his family. In the same breath he asked, "Where is everybody?"

Mr. McGovern hesitated for a minute and took a deep breath. "You have some relatives in California who were having difficulties. Your father went out there to try to help them. The government detained him, and they wouldn't let him contact anyone. Your mother and Billy went to find him, and they were also detained. Since she couldn't contact you, Sam, she sent me this letter."

He reached out to open a little drawer in the table next to his chair. Producing Mother's letter, he said, "It seems that your relatives couldn't speak English that well and didn't understand what was happening. They were detained along with your family. Your mother asked me to watch your house and keep in touch with Sarah."

Sam was physically shaken and couldn't discuss it anymore. He knew that he would have to try to find them. Changing the subject, he asked about Mickey. Mrs. McGovern said, "Oh, she's fine. She's in college, doing fine, majoring in her favorite subject, biology."

Mr. McGovern interrupted her and said, "It's very lonely around here with everybody gone." He was looking at a large picture on the wall of Tom and Sam after winning the cross-country race. Glancing back at Sam with tears in his eyes and his voice breaking up slightly, he said, "You know he loved you." Sam remained speechless. They sat there meditating for a few minutes.

Sam thought, *He was always ready to throw a block for me. The last one cost him his life. I will never forgive those bastards responsible for taking him away from us.*

Sam asked about Sarah. Mr. McGovern told him that she was in a sanitarium; however, she was doing well and Stan was with her constantly. After receiving the address of the institution from them, Sam said good-bye graciously and asked them to send his regards to Mickey. He left, deeply shocked and confused. Not knowing exactly what to do next, he decided to visit Sarah.

The sanitarium was a short distance from town. As he entered the building, his heart sank at the thought of Sarah's anguish. When he approached her room, the door was open. He entered unnoticed and saw Stan sitting at the side of her bed with his back to the door. He was holding her hand and saying, "Sarah, if you don't get better soon, I'll be too old to make love to you."

She opened her eyes slowly. Gently smiling, she said, "No, you won't."

They finally realized that they weren't alone and noticed Sam. The three of them broke into laughter. It was like old times. They enjoyed each other's company, and Sam felt some of the tension ease. His sister was going to get well, and Stan would always be there for her.

After an hour or so, Sam asked Stan if he or Sarah had any contact with his parents. They both shook their heads indicating that they hadn't. Then Stan suddenly asked Sarah, "The letter! What happened to the letter you got from your mother?" Sarah pointed to a drawer next to her bed. Stan pulled it open, found the letter, and gave it to Sam.

"That's it. All she says is that your father is being detained along with your uncle. There's something about their being involved in an organization suspected of disloyalty. She and Billy will stay with him until it's straightened out. That was the last contact we had with them. The phone number in the letter is out of operation, and all the letters that Sarah and I sent were returned." He produced them from the same drawer for Sam to see. "It seems as though they just vanished."

Sam thought for a while and then said, "I don't understand. The only organization that Father was ever involved in was the Japanese language school that he sent me to. What could that possibly have to do with disloyalty? It was my ability to speak and understand the language so thoroughly that helped this country break the Japanese code, making it possible for us to gain an advantage over the enemy and further enabling us to overpower them in one of the most important battles of the war.

"Those schools provided America with a valuable resource, teaching thousands of Americans to speak and understand the Japanese language. They're out there right now, all over the Pacific, working as interpreters and doing combat intelligence work, helping to kill tens of thousands of Japanese. What the hell is this all about? How can my father be accused of disloyalty? I'm sorry, Stan. I didn't mean to get so carried away. This whole thing is getting to me."

Stan replied, "It's okay. We understand. Sarah and I have been going through this for months. If you find out anything, contact me at my parents' home and I'll inform Sarah."

Sam shook his hand and thanked him again. He said good-bye and left them the way that he found them—together.

After he left Sarah and Stan, Sam felt cold and alone. His head ached. It had been a long day. He checked into a small hotel in town. With a strong sense of helplessness, he descended into deep despair. His mind was full of questions. *Where do I start? Should I go to California? Then what? Do I knock on doors? What doors? If they're locking up Japs, would they think that I was a spy in a naval uniform?* Looking at the phone on the nightstand, he thought of calling someone. *Who? A congressman, the attorney general, the FBI?* A terrible feeling of urgency settled in and he felt as though his body was ready to explode.

The thoughts shooting through his brain were like slippery eels. He tried to hold on to one, but he was becoming more and more confused. Then he remembered the phone. Maybe there was only one person that could help. He reached out to turn on the lamp near the bed. It gave off a dim, eerie glow. Straining his eyes to see the time on his watch, he saw that it read 9:35 p.m. Perfect. It would be five hours earlier, making it 4:35 p.m., Hawaii time. He might still be able to reach Harlin Cooper, his commander.

Nervously, his fingers turned the dial. When the operator asked, "Can I help you?" Sam remembered the feeling going through his body. He wanted to yell out, "Yes, help me! Help me!" Snapping back to reality, he said, "Please, Hawaii. I have to call Hawaii." Giving her the information, he told her to ask for Commander Harlin Cooper.

The operator asked, "Who shall I say is calling?"

Expecting to hear an important name, she was probably disappointed when he answered, "Sam Sagarra."

It seemed to take forever. He could hear someone answer. There was a lot of broken conversations going on between the operator and the other end in Hawaii. Suddenly, he heard Harlin's powerful voice.

"Hello, who is this?"

"It's Sam Sagarra, sir," he yelled back.

The connection must have been breaking up because the commander asked again, "Who?"

"Sam, Sam Sagarra," he replied again.

Finally, the commander recognized him. "Oh, Sagarra, where the hell are you?"

Sam told him everything. If Harlin believed in half of what he had preached to Sam, he would help him if he could. Sam poured out his heart to his commander. Harlin was sympathetic and said he would try to help.

Before hanging up, he asked Sam where he was staying. After he gave him the information, Commander Cooper said in a forceful tone, "*Stay put!* It will take me a while, but I'll get back to you."

When Sam hung up the phone, he felt relieved. He thought, *Harlin had actually seemed shocked when I told him about my parents. He might be a friend after all, someone who would really help.* He rested his head on the pillow and closed his weary eyes. His mind finally at rest, Sam fell asleep.

Sam stayed in that room for two days. Afraid to leave, he felt like a caged animal. His brain had a photo image of every crack in the ceiling, and he was starting to count the cracks on the wall. Suddenly the phone rang, startling him. He jumped out of bed and picked up the receiver. The commander's gruff voice greeted him.

"Sam? Sam, are you there?" Once again they were yelling at each other over a bad connection. With every other word disappearing, Sam was finally able to make out what Harlin was saying. "They're in California at Santa Anita."

Sam yelled back, "Santa Anita. That's a racetrack. What the hell would they be doing at a racetrack? Are you sure?"

His commander replied, "Yes, Sam. I thought that I didn't hear it correctly either, but that's the answer I got. Look, California is on your way back here. You have a few weeks left, and I'm trying to get you another two. You deserve it. Stay in touch."

Sam thanked him and hung up.

CHAPTER 21

That evening Sam was on a plane to California. On arrival the next day he took a taxi. When he told the driver to take him to Santa Anita racetrack, the driver gave him a peculiar look.

Knowing, because of his attire, that he had just flown in, the driver asked, "Don't you know that the track is closed? There is no racing this time of year."

Sam replied, "I came to find my parents."

Realizing his stupidity, the driver started the motor and they drove off.

When they arrived at the track, he slowed down, letting Sam out at the front entrance. Sam stood there for a while, absorbing the sight. He couldn't believe his eyes. Guards holding machine guns were on patrol at the closed gate. *What did Father do?* he thought. Sam felt as though he was coming to visit someone in prison.

Approaching the guards, he could see the curiosity in the soldiers' eyes. Sam could imagine what was probably going through their minds. *We've got these Japs locked in here trying to get out, and this one wants to get in.* After showing his ID, they admitted him.

This place stinks was his very first thought. *Why would my family be put in here?*

Immediately upon entering, there was a sign pointing to the Reception and Information Center. The lady behind the desk was Japanese, and Sam inquired if there was a family named Sagarra detained there. After checking her files, she came back and said, "Yes, written on the card is section twenty-one, room sixty-seven." His heart was throbbing as he walked and ran toward section twenty-one. Slowing down to read the room numbers, he realized that they weren't rooms at all. They were horse stalls. He thought that the receptionist had made a mistake. However, there were children running around. A little boy was playing ball, and the young girls were jumping rope. He continued on to stall sixty-seven.

Hesitating for a second before entering, he looked in. The stall was full of people. Suddenly, from somewhere in that crowd, a beautiful lady broke free. Running to him and almost knocking him down, she threw her arms around his neck. Squeezing tightly, she started to cry uncontrollably.

In between sobs, his mother kept repeating his name. "Sam, Sam, we heard about the battles over there. We thought that you were dead." Tightening her grip around his neck, she cried, "I thought I'd never see you again."

They stood there for a few minutes holding each other when suddenly, almost as Mother had done, Father and Billy came bursting out of the crowd. The four of them just hung on to each other. They were all afraid to let go—afraid that if they did, they might wake up and find out that it was only a dream.

Eventually, they regained control of their emotions. Mother, holding Sam's hand, led him to one side of the stable. They walked behind a curtain that had been hung for privacy reasons.

Sam asked, "Mother, who are all these people?"

She replied, "They were all strangers that arrived at the same time we did." "But, there's seven people in here," Sam said. The stable was approximately the size of an eighteen-by-twenty-foot compartment.

She explained further, "They don't allot rooms according to the amount of people. They assign two families to each room." She insisted on calling that stable a room. "Some families have five or six people each. Therefore, some rooms house ten or eleven people."

Sam was horrified. Looking around, he said, "There's no bathroom."

Father replied, "Everyone has to use outhouses, a few for each section."

"Yeah," Billy added, "and they contain some terrible smelling chemical that burns your eyes while you're—"

Mother put her hand over Billy's mouth to keep him from becoming more descriptive.

There obviously was no electricity because of the multitude of candles being utilized. Their cots had mattresses stuffed with straw obtained from the stables. They reeked.

Sam asked Father, "How many people are in this place?"

Taking a moment to consider, he answered, "I heard last week that the number was about six thousand."

Shocked, Sam replied, "What? Six thousand? I didn't think that they could keep more than three hundred horses here in good health. How can they possible keep six thousand people healthy, especially without good sanitary conditions? This is totally inhuman! Complete insanity!"

Sam finally settled down. Mother made room for him to stay over, squeezing him in between Billy and the wall. He felt like a canned sardine sleeping on a filthy straw mattress. They spent the next few days catching up and enjoying each other's company. They weren't allowed to send or receive any mail. Sam tried to bring them up to date. However, since he had been out of contact, his information was limited. They discussed Sarah. Sam told them that she was almost well and that she and Stan planned to get married.

Mother asked, "Have you heard from Charlie?"

Sam replied, "The last time I heard from him was in a letter I received a week before I went on special duty. Charlie said that everything was fine. He was with a great bunch of guys, and he was happy. After that, my company was restricted by a communication blackout. Even you couldn't reach me."

When Mother and Sam were alone, Sam questioned, "How is Father?" Besides being a proud man, Father was also a good actor, always pretending that everything was fine—even when it wasn't.

Mother answered, "I don't know, Sam. It's always hard to tell with him, although this time he can't hide it. He is very hurt and disillusioned. They destroyed his business, raped his daughter, and told his children that they're not good enough to be American. Now this ultimate disgrace! They have taken away his honor."

She started to cry, and Sam took her frail, shaking body in his arms, telling her he would try to do something. He thought, *Maybe Commander Cooper can help.* Then he silently debated with himself. *He's so far away. What could he do? However, I will try because, at this point, Cooper is the only friend I have.*

Trying to get through to Hawaii, with a five-hour time difference, was a task in itself. Calling from a phone that was nailed onto a pole, with six thousand people chattering around him, was an unequivocal challenge. When Sam finally reached Commander Cooper, they had to yell at each other again. The commander seemed to be having more difficulty hearing than he was. Sam thought, *Maybe the reason he can't hear me is because I'm chewing gum.* Taking it out of his mouth, he stuck the gum on the pole. It did make a slight difference. Now the commander could understand Sam, but with all the surrounding noise, Sam couldn't hear him. Jamming his finger in one ear and listening to the phone with other one still didn't remedy the situation. Glancing at the gum stuck to the pole, he got an idea. He pulled it off and stuck it in his ear. It worked, successfully blocking the noise. He felt as though he was in a submarine, but at least he could hear Commander Cooper.

After Sam described the living conditions and the guards with machine guns at the front gate, the commander went crazy. He bellowed, "I don't understand why they're still keeping them locked up! There ain't no more danger to the coast. The marines have landed on Guadalcanal. We got those Ja … sorry, Sam, bastards on the run. They should let 'em all go. Sam, they told me it was only temporary. Anyway, why don't you come on back? We'll see what we can do from here."

Sam replied, "Thank you, sir," and hung up. He didn't feel any better than before, but he knew he couldn't do anything about it. Things would have to take their course. He would have to leave. Maybe everything would work itself out. After a long and tearful good-bye, Sam was on his way back to Hawaii.

CHAPTER 22

COMING BACK TO HAWAII was like landing on another planet. Sam was still unable to come to terms with what he had seen. A few days after returning, Commander Cooper sent for him. As he entered headquarters, Lieutenant Hugh Martin was just coming out of the control room. Noticing him, Hugh said, "Hi, Sam. Glad to see that you're in one piece. Heard you just visited hell." Sam just looked at him as he continued speaking. "The commander's been telling me what they've done to your family. Go on in. He's been waiting to see you."

As he walked in, Sam saluted.

In his heavy, gruff voice, the commander greeted him. "Sam. C'mon in, son." Analyzing Sam with his eyes, he said, "I'd say you look like shit, but that's too good. Pull up a chair." The commander showed him a chart. "I have a special assignment for you. But first give me the lowdown on your family."

Hesitating, Sam sadly said, "Sir, I don't know where to start. If you didn't see it with your own eyes, you couldn't believe that it's really happening. Not here! Not in America. They're being treated worse than prisoners. They won't let them communicate with the outside world. There's no sanitary facilities. They stand in line over an hour for some kind of smelly soup and potato, and the housing is awful. Two families share a horse stall, usually ten to twelve people, sleeping on smelly, straw-filled mattresses. They had to stuff the mattresses themselves with the straw from the floor of the stall. It seems like they just moved a few hundred horses out and moved thousands of people in—"

The commander interrupted, "Sam, I was told that it's only temporary. They're supposed to move them to a better place soon."

"Sir," Sam replied, "they're being treated worse than animals now! How much better can it get? In fact, some congressman is even suggesting that the women be sterilized and the men castrated."

The commander interrupted again in a bragging Texas drawl. "Ya know, Sam, in Texas we cut the balls off the little heifers so they don't chase the cows around. They just mosey along, getting big and fat. I'm an expert at it. If I hear about anything like that goin' on, we'll take this whole damn company back there and find that fuckin' congressman. We'll tie a rope around the bastard's balls and attach the other end to one of my Texas longhorn steers. I'll show him what it really feels like to be castrated!" Starting to chuckle, he continued, "Then we'll roast the bastard's balls over an open fire and eat them. You should try them sometime."

As he burst into uncontrollable laughter, he paused only to exclaim, "They're great!! Listen, son, I know that this has been a bad time for you, but you have to take a break. Get your mind going in another direction. Give it a rest."

Getting back to the special assignment he wanted to discuss with Sam, the commander said, "The marines are going after one of the small outer islands. Reports say the enemy is using it as a staging area.

They've got enough firepower stored on it to blow themselves to kingdom come, and we're gonna help 'em do it."

Sam asked, "Sir, what do they need me for? I'm not a marine."

The commander replied, "The interpreters that the marines have are good, but you're the best! You understand the language so well. You wouldn't have a hard time convincing someone that you were born in Japan and lived there your whole life. The marines can't take a chance with this one. They have asked for help, and I'm sending you. It'll do ya good. Put your brain back to work."

As Sam left the commander's office, he thought, *It isn't my brain that I'm worried about.* The thought of going to a Japanese island, converted to a munitions storage facility and staging area, wasn't exactly what Sam had envisioned his participation in this war would be. *I want to fly. Instead I'll be crawling up on some wet beach leading an attack, with thousands of marines shooting up my ass.*

For the next few days, Sam attended briefings and orientation meetings with his marine counterparts, five Japanese guys like him. All of them had American first names and had been born in the United States. The group included Louie Yoshimo, Mike Sasaki, Dan Kusumo, Harry Masaka, and Bobby Nakaoma. All but the last two came from the West Coast. Their families were also in concentration camps around the country. Harry Masaka and Bobby Nakaoma came from Hawaii, and their families were unaffected.

Another thing they had in common was that they had all learned to speak Japanese by attending Japanese language schools. Now there was a desperate need for Americans who could speak Japanese fluently. People like Sam's father and uncle were in jail for supporting the schools that taught these interpreters. Sam thought, *Has this whole damn world gone crazy, or is it just me?*

One week later, Sam was on a landing craft with his newly acquired Japanese buddies. Accompanied by thousands of marines, they stormed the beaches. From the start he had a premonition that it wasn't going to be their day. Everyone was aboard amphibians that stopped very close to the beach. Finally Sam's craft stopped, the landing gate went down, and someone yelled, "Okay, guys, go."

All six of them jumped out and disappeared in seven feet of water, just a slight miscalculation. Fortunately, the equipment was packed in waterproof containers. As they hit the beach, it was like one hell of a Fourth of July celebration. There was only one major difference: the fireworks were aimed at them.

It took them four hours to reach the edge of the jungle. Due to the ricocheting bullets, the enemy couldn't get a good bead on them, but the mosquitoes were right on target. Sam pictured more guys getting transfusions for the loss of blood because of mosquitoes than as the result of being shot. There wasn't a part of them that escaped being bitten by the swarm of diving insects. However, they were luckier than the guys in front. Those guys apparently had fallen into a swamp infested with leeches. Hearing the screams and cursing, Sam's group changed its course. Luckily the heavy equipment had slowed them down; otherwise, they would have been in the leech pond as well.

Having passed the enemy's first line of defense, they advanced about a quarter of a mile through dense jungle. Coming to a line of tall trees, they stopped to regroup. The trees made good cover. If they could get an antenna up near the top of one of those trees, they would be able to scan most of the island. Mike Sasaki volunteered for the job. He had to climb up and down while exposed to enemy fire. About a hundred rounds of bullets were fired at him. However, the gods must have been with him because he did the job and got down in one piece.

The rest of the company spread out, flanking them on both sides. The strategy was to try to pick up some conversation, enabling them to zero in on the enemy's position. They immediately got the wires hooked up and put the earphones on. They were in business! Silence dominated as though the enemy was waiting for them to make the next move.

After what seemed to be an eternity, they started to pick up some chattering. Sam was just beginning to pinpoint the location. As he rose to get the lieutenant's attention, suddenly some rapid fire opened up to the right of him. He felt a sharp pain ripping through his body as a bullet entered his chest, nailing him against the tree with such force that he felt as though he had become part of it. As the soldier who shot him appeared, Sam yelled, "Hold your fire. Don't shoot anymore. I'm on your side. We're the reconnaissance group."

The American soldier just stood there horrified as three other soldiers ran up from behind him. One of them quickly put a temporary bandage on Sam to stop the bleeding. He exclaimed, "Holy shit! I can't believe we shot our own guys."

While the others shouted for the medics, the soldier who arrived first finally said hysterically, "I'm sorry. I'm sorry. I thought I was shooting at the enemy."

Sam, straining to speak, sarcastically responded, "Don't let it bother you. Maybe you were." The soldier appeared puzzled at his response. Sam angrily exclaimed, "Just help me get the fuck out of here!"

Blinded with pain, Sam hadn't noticed that Mike Sasaki, who survived climbing up and down the tree with the whole Japanese arming shooting at him, was also shot by one of their own guys. The soldier who shot Mike also claimed that he mistook him for the enemy. The only problem with the soldier's excuse was that he and Mike had been together since training camp.

CHAPTER 23

Sam was sent back to Hawaii and spent the next six months in the hospital recuperating. The doctors could not remove the bullet. When they operated, it was found embedded in the back of his ribs, too close to the spinal cord. Trying to extricate the bullet could have caused permanent paralysis, so Sam had this memento to carry with him for the rest of his life.

While fighting for his country, Sam was shot by one of his own guys with an American bullet, but he finally did get a chance to fly. After his recuperation period was over, he went up with his squadron. Suddenly a group of enemy planes appeared, and a dogfight ensued. The American planes were going down like crazy, and Sam had a zero on his tail that he couldn't shake. In an attempt to lose him, he flew into a cloud bank. As he reemerged, the zero was flying right beside him, so close that Sam could see his eyes. The pilot had a terribly confused expression on his face as he stared back at him. He didn't know what to make of a Japanese pilot flying an American plane. He couldn't make up his mind whether or not he should wave or shoot him down. Apparently unable to decide, he banked off to the right and disappeared. He reappeared suddenly in front of Sam, coming straight at him, and the two planes collided head on.

Sam could feel the burning body of the other pilot wrapped around him. Spinning wildly out of control, they fell from the sky, hitting the ground with a fiery explosion. Thrown free, Sam opened his eyes. He was horrified when he realized that the other pilot's dead body was wrapped around him. The mutilated, burnt face was pressed against his. He struggled desperately to get free from the scorched corpse.

"Sam! Sam! Wake up! Wake up!"

The night nurse awakened him. Covered with perspiration, Sam realized the whole episode was a nightmare. That nightmare would repeat constantly for the next few years.

After a few months in the hospital, Sam was visited by Louie Yoshimo. Out on furlough, he came to Hawaii to look up Sam. Louie told him, "Sam, you were lucky."

Oddly, Sam didn't share that sentiment.

"A few hours after you left, all hell let loose," Louie said. "They threw everything they had at us. Then it started to rain. When the rain stopped, the mosquitoes were back in droves. The artillery kept firing at us through it all. The mud was so deep that if a shell hit one of the guys, he was blown apart and buried all in one action. Half of them couldn't be found when we were evacuated."

Sam asked, "How about the other guys from our recon group?"

Louie said, "Just me, Sam. I'm the only one who got off that island in one piece. It took us four weeks to get halfway up that hill. All the way we encountered local islanders hidden in caves, who wouldn't come out. Danny Kusumo went into one of the caves to try to coax the people to come out.

"There was an enemy soldier hiding among them. He shot Danny in the head and half of the locals for allowing him to come in. The other half of the locals came running out. They were all yelling at the same time, trying to tell us what happened. I understood them and asked if anyone was still alive in there. One of the locals replied, 'Only Japanese soldier.'

"I went in to try to convince him to give himself up. Danny was face down, the earth around his head soaked with blood. I noticed some movement at the back of the cave and pleaded to whomever it was to come out. I told him in Japanese that he wouldn't be harmed. Suddenly, out of the darkness, this guy came charging at me. Apparently out of ammo, he tried to take out my guts with his bayonet. I reacted instinctively, jumping out of his path. As he went by, I hit him with my rifle butt, cracking the back of his skull open. He fell right next to Danny. As he lay there dying, the blood of the two soldiers ran together. A spiritual feeling shot through my body, giving me the chills. It was as though they were holding hands like two brothers on their way to heaven."

Louie continued, "When I came out of the cave, there was a whole lot of screaming going on. There was a girl standing at the edge of a cliff, intending to jump. From what I could make out, it seemed that her whole family had been killed in the cave by the same guy who shot Danny. I pushed through the crowd, thinking that maybe I could help talk her out of suicide. I froze when she stared at me. I didn't want her to think I was going to hurt her. Stopping about ten feet in front of her, our eyes locked together. She was the most beautiful girl that I had ever seen. I just wanted to put my arms around her and hold her forever. After a few moments, I began talking softly in Japanese, pleading with her not to kill herself, to take my hand, and that I would protect her. She seemed to be so confused, and I could see her eyes becoming watery. As large tears started streaming down her cheeks, I thought I had her, Sam!

"Suddenly, as though she had changed her mind, the girl began shaking her head. Still looking at me, she said in an unbelievable tone of voice, 'No, no. You are the devil.' She quickly turned and jumped off the cliff."

Tears built up in his eyes as he continued, "I tried to grab her, but she slipped through my fingers." After regaining his composure, he said, "A piece of my heart went off that cliff with her, Sam."

Louie changed the subject before he broke down completely. "Harry Masaka and Bobby Nakaoma both got shoulder wounds. Fortunately they weren't chopped up too badly. They'll be okay. Every time we stuck our heads out, we drew fire from the Japanese in front and our own guys hit us from the sides and rear. They later apologized, saying we looked like the enemy. We were lucky all of us weren't killed."

Louie left soon after wishing Sam well and saying, "I hope we will meet again." As it turned out, twenty years after the war, their paths would cross again.

Before leaving the hospital, Sam received a letter from his brother Charlie. It started off, "Dear Sam …" Then Charlie quickly apologized for calling Sam "dear." He had a quirk about calling anyone dear, other than the female gender.

Sam was happy to hear from him because Charlie was not much of a writer. Communicating with each other had been next to impossible. Being separated by two oceans made it even more difficult. Charlie's company was never in one place long enough. They were continuously on the move, doing the impossible.

Charlie described a battle that he had just been through in Italy. "Sam, these Nazis ran across Europe like a stampeding herd of buffalo, storming forward in high gear. Suddenly they collided with us. Slowly but surely we're making 'em turn and go the other way. They sure are stubborn bastards. We pushed a whole company of Nazis about ten miles through heavy woods, and we were sure that we had them on the run when suddenly they turned and came right at us. We held our ground, throwing everything we had at them. Most of them stopped and turned back. However, about one hundred crazy Nazis kept right on coming. One of 'em passed by so fast, he didn't even notice me. I caught him with a grenade that landed between the back of his neck and his backpack, blowing his head clean off. Four others took mortar hits at close range, blowing them to pieces no more than ten feet in front of me. It was a fuckin' mess. There were arms, legs, and other body parts landing all around me. A head, with its helmet still on, rol led right between my legs. It was awful!"

Sam laid back and continued reading his brother's letter. "The guys that I'm with are mostly Japanese. We've had a lot of casual ties in the past year and lost some really good men. This is where we want to be, right up on the front line. The weather has been nasty and cold for this time of year. Fortunately, I have some hot-blooded Italian beauties to keep me warm on those frosty nights.

"We're just about finished here in Italy. From what I hear, we'll be on our way to France in a few weeks. They're having trouble with some other stubborn Nazis, so they invited us to come over and do some ass kickin'. I'm looking forward to meeting some of those great French women. I have six months to go before my birthday, but I expect to start celebrating early. Take care of yourself, Sam. Your brother, Charlie."

As Sam read Charlie's letter, one part made him very curious. *Out there on the front line, in the middle of the woods, where did he find those hot-blooded Italian women?*" However, he thought about it further, *If he's my same old brother Charlie, his front line always has a fifty-mile radius.*

CHAPTER 24

ABOUT SIX WEEKS AFTER Sam was released from the hospital, Lieutenant Hugh Martin came to visit him in his barracks. Sam had not seen him since being discharged from the hospital. They spent a few minutes talking about how he was getting back into things. Then Hugh began excusing himself, saying, "I'm on my way to a meeting." The lieutenant looked back, pausing as though he had forgotten something, and said, "Oh, Sam, I told Commander Cooper I was coming out this way. He wanted me to stop by and ask you to report to headquarters as soon as possible."

Sam thanked him as he left.

Sam made himself presentable and left immediately. As he walked toward headquarters, his mind was full of questions. What was he going to do now? What other crazy assignment or mundane task was he going to be assigned to? When he entered the building, there were none of the normal greetings. With the combination of his special assignments and his personal problems, Sam was in and out of the commander's office so many times that everyone got to know him.

He had become sort of a regular and was always greeted with funny little quips.

Today all he got was a solemn "Hi, Sam" and "Hi, Sagarra." They all seemed to know where he was headed. No one asked him anything or tried to stop him. He walked up and knocked on Cooper's door.

In his burly voice, the commander said, "Come in." Seeing him, Cooper said, "Sam, come on in and pull up a chair."

He could see that the commander was distressed, and Sam became concerned. He couldn't imagine what Cooper had for him now.

In a solemn and slightly broken voice, the commander said, "Son, on days like today, I would give anything not to be who I am. I'm a very proud man and, at the same time, a very sad one. There was a battle a few weeks ago."

Looking at Sam, he could see that he was becoming more concerned and confused. He continued, "The battle had nothing to do with the navy. It was fought in France "—his voice became stronger— "b y a combat team of Japanese Americans. They broke through the lines of battle-hardened Nazi troops that had surrounded a battalion of about three hundred Texans and saved their lives. This combat team accomplished a next-to-impossible feat, but they paid dearly for iit. The casualty numbers were high, more than fifty per cent.

"I was informed about the battle in a letter written by a Texas congressman, whom I've been friendly with since our grade school days. They want to make the whole bunch of them honorary citizens of Texas." Holding the letter out so that Sam could see it, the commander said, "I received this letter a week ago. I was hoping I wouldn't need to have this conversation with you. However, today I received another letter." Pausing for a second, he handed the letter to Sam. "It's from the War Department. I'm so sorry to have to give you this news."

Dazed, Sam took it from him. He didn't know how long he sat there. He didn't remember saying anything as he left. Sam just walked slowly back to his barracks. He sat on his cot with the letter, still unopened, in his hand. Burying his head into his hands, he began to cry hysterically. His body began to tighten and quiver as the shock of this terrible tragedy took control of his mind.

A desperate need to be held by someone came over him. He wanted somebody to hold him close and tell him that everything was going to be okay and tomorrow would be a better day. He started thinking irrationally. If he didn't open the letter, he wouldn't be able to read about Charlie's death. If he didn't read about it, maybe Char lie would still be alive and come home someday.

He fell into a deeply disturbed sleep with visions of Charlie and Tommy going through his mind all night. He saw his parents being kept behind bars by a country that their son had just died for. When Sam awoke, he was still clutching the unopened letter.

As it turned out, Sam would never open it. He would keep it in a glass container on his desk to remind him of Charlie and his life at that time. It was a little more than a year after Charlie's death when America dropped the atomic bomb on Japan, ending the war. The celebration went on for weeks. Everyone began making preparations to go home. Some of the guys decided to have one more fling, a going-away party. Lieutenant Martin insisted that Sam join them. When he turned him down, the lieutenant exclaimed, "I'm ordering you to join us!" Laughing, he continued, "Sam, we've been stuck out here together for over four years. We've gone through some pretty rough times. Let's finish it over a drink."

Sam agreed.

They went to a few places. Each one had its own party going on. Music was blasting, everyone was dancing, and each guy had to have two girls. It definitely had to be a soldiers' version of what heaven was like.

They finally ended up in a quaint little bar on Umu Street in downtown Honolulu. By the time they arrived there, Sam had already had too much to drink, and he was feeling woozy.

When Lieutenant Martin ordered another round of drinks, Sam thought he refused but probably drank it anyway. He was feeling no pain. There was a little dance floor, and a few girls were wandering around. Lieutenant Martin motioned for the girls to join them. After they introduced themselves, the girls sat down at their table. They spent the next few hours talking and dancing, interwoven with more drinking. When it came close to closing time, the bartender announced, "The last drinks are on the house!" Sam thought that the last drink felt like he had put the whole house in it. Not being wimpy servicemen and wanting to impress their newfound lady friends, they drained their glasses. That was the last thing Sam remembered.

The next morning he awoke to a stream of light in his face. It was the same stream of light that woke him up every morning, except this morning Sam felt a little strange. The normal back pain that he arose with every morning was gone. In fact, his whole body felt great! He wanted to turn over, but his head refused to move.

He couldn't figure out why it didn't hurt. It just felt as though his head was filled with lead. As his brain started to clear slightly, Sam noticed something else quite unusual. There seemed to be someone sharing his cot. He thought, *Surely, my mind must be playing tricks on me. My cot has barely enough room for me.*

As his senses started returning, he finally realized this bed was too soft to be his cot. Panic set in, but his head still felt like lead, making it difficult to turn around. He slowly reached back in a sort of exploring motion, and his hand landed on a mound. Continuing to explore, his hand traveled down into a valley and up again. He was shocked into reality. There was a woman in his bed, or he was in her bed. He had no idea where he was. Miraculously, the heaviness in his head dissipated. He sat up quickly, startling her awake with his abrupt movement.

She asked, "What's wrong?"

He momentarily couldn't speak. No words would come out of his mouth. All he could think about was how extremely beautiful she was. There was no doubt in his mind that he had died and gone to heaven. He was in bed with a gorgeous Japanese woman. Her beautiful half-awake eyes were partially covered by her long, luxurious black hair. That magnificent hair gently rolled over her shoulders in front of her breasts, somewhat covering her sumptuous naked body.

Regaining his composure, he asked, "Who are you?"

She replied softly, "I am Nuokei."

Looking into her eyes, Sam asked doubtfully, "Did I do anything?"

Nuokei answered disappointedly, "If you cannot remember, I will not tell you."

He hesitated for a second and then asked, "Did I hurt you?"

Nuokei sat up and rolled over to get closer to him. She pushed him down on the bed, lying across him with her breasts on his chest. To help her portray what she was about to describe, she gently placed her hand, as though it was a claw, on his stomach. Continuing downward with a slow circular motion, she paused and said, "You were like a lion with a very large cub, licking and nuzzling my breasts until they were on fire. Then, with your claws, you forced my thighs apart." To add some intrigue to her story, she lowered her hand and buried her nails like little daggers firmly into his groin.

After pausing for effect, she continued, "Your large cub crawled through the forest and entered my den, roaring for hours within its walls. Reaching its crescendo, our juices flowed together. I could still feel its strong throbbing inside of me as we fell asleep in each other's arms."

Sam stupidly replied that he didn't remember any of that.

Full of anger and frustration, she berated him, "How can you not remember spending an evening filled with such delight?" In a disgusted voice, she shouted, "Then you and your little cub can leave now!"

Suddenly she jumped out of bed and, with the strength of an angered boar, dragged him out of bed. She pushed him across the room. Angrily, she opened the door and threw him out of the apartment into the hallway, slamming the door shut with a thunderous bang that almost shattered his eardrums. As the shocked neighbors stared at him, Sam realized that he was standing out there completely nude. He banged on her door, pleading for his clothes.

From behind the closed door, she yelled, "No. You go back to base naked! You show your lieutenant what kind of fuckin' dummy you are."

Sam continued to plead with her, and after a while she relented. Opening the door, she threw his clothes at him. In disgust she quickly slammed it shut again.

CHAPTER 25

WITHIN A FEW MONTHS, Sam received his discharge papers. The reality of the war ending finally started to take hold. Pertinent questions flooded his mind. *Where is my home? Where will I go? Back to Chicago? What will it be like?*

He had received a letter from Sarah. She and Stan were married. They did not go to New York as Stan had previously planned. Instead they remained in Chicago. McGovern needed someone to fill a position at the bank, and Stan filled the bill. Jack had made Stan an offer that he couldn't refuse. With McGovern's help, they were able to keep and maintain the family home. Sarah's letter also mentioned Mother and Father. They were going to be released any day now and would return with a few thousand other families, who were being relocated in Chicago. However, to Mother and Father, this was coming home. The letter closed with Stan sending his regards. He added that they were going to be parents in seven months. "Come home soon. We all will be waiting for you, Uncle Sam. Love, Sarah."

Sam arrived in Chicago three months later. His heart started pounding, and the excitement built up inside of him as Sam approached his home. His whole body started to shake in anticipation of shortly being together again with his family. It was like a dream. After all the years of undescribable misery and horror, he thought, *I truly believed that I would never see any of them again*. As he entered the house, Mother was coming out of the living room, carrying a handful of magazines. At first, when she saw him, she was startled as though she was seeing a ghost. Then, dropping the magazines, she ran to him with her arms outstretched. They stood there, mother and son, tightly embracing in an emotional sea of tears.

As they parted, Mother, still crying and sobbing between words, said, "Sam, I thought I would only see you again in my dreams."

Sam could see the horror of the past few years had left its mark on her. Now there were thin streaks of gray shooting through her hair, which had once been a vibrant jet black. Her face was drawn but smooth, and her walk still had a little bounce left in it. Mother was a survivor! She was alive and ready to tackle the task of rebuilding their lives.

Taking Sam by the hand, she led him down the hall. "Come, Father is working in the backyard."

They walked out onto the porch. He could see Father on his knees, pruning his rose bushes. They had always referred to them as "Father's roses" because they were different from any other flowers they had ever seen. The roses were the size of large grapefruits, the petals capturing every color of the rainbow.

When Father finally noticed that he was being observed, he looked up, squinting and straining his eyes in disbelief. He jumped to his feet and ran up onto the porch. Hesitating for a second with his pruning shears still in his hand, he threw his arms around Sam's neck, and Sam hugged his father. Completely ignoring all Japanese tradition, they held each other, squeezing tighter as if signifying they would never let go again.

They spent the next couple of weeks filling in the gaps of the years of separation. When Father and Sam began serious discussions of their plans for the future, Father became slightly withdrawn, as though he had already made his decision. Hesitating to gather the right words, he said, "I have not seen your grandfather for many years. We only recently heard he has survived the war. I think I would like to go home and spend some time with him. I have come to a fork in the road of my life. Maybe there I will be able to decide which road to take. I believe that here, in this country, there is nothing for me."

It was the first time Sam had ever heard him refer to Japan as "home." He knew in his heart that if Father did leave, he would never return.

A few weeks later, they were all invited to have dinner with the McGoverns at their home. The years away created a large hole in their lives, but Jack McGovern and Father had a relationship that no amount of time could deteriorate. After dinner, they returned to the living room where everyone engaged in a conversation about the future.

Jack glanced over at Father and asked, "Do you intend to go back into business as before?" He graciously offered his help if Father needed it.

Before replying, Father took one of his deep, thoughtful, decisive breaths. "My son Charlie was killed in Europe. The country he died for didn't have enough respect for him to even notify his parents. We only learned about it when we were released. He had already been dead for over a year and a half. Charlie gave his life to save thousands of American strangers. They took it willingly, and in return his America, which he died for, destroyed the honor of his parents —humiliating and disgracing the rest of his family, locking us up behind barbed wire fences with armed guards on twenty-four-hour duty."

As his eyes became glassy, Father realized he was pouring his heart out to Jack and immediately apologized.

After taking a sip from a drink he had just poured for himself, Jack McGovern turned back to Father and said, "I know that it's foolish for me or anyone to say we understand." He took another sip of his drink and continued, "No one will ever feel or fully understand what all of you went through. They won't even be able to make sense of it. However, I would like you to know"—he looked directly at Father—"that I will always be here if you need me."

Father thanked Jack with the deepest gratitude. "You have always been there for me, giving me the sincerest friendship and having faith in me. Nevertheless, I feel that I must return to my roots. Japan could use a few friends now. Maybe there I will find a place for myself."

Sam broke in and asked about Mickey. Mrs. McGovern replied, "Mickey's doing fine. She's finished college and is working at a biological research facility."

Sam remarked, "That's what she always wanted to do. She loved biology." He paused for a second and then asked, "Is she seeing anyone?"

Mrs. McGovern solemnly and apologetically replied, "Yes, she is, Sam."

Sam told Mrs. McGovern to give her his regards and that he wished her well. It was getting late so they all said good night and left.

CHAPTER 26

BY THE END OF the following month, Father's mind was made up. He was going back to Japan, and Sam, not having any reason to stay in America, decided to accompany him. During the next six months, they sold what little was left, giving the house to Sarah and Stan. The four of them were off. Mother, Father, Billy, and Sam left on a ship heading for Japan.

Father and Mother felt as though they were going home, but for Billy and Sam, it was a voyage to a strange and mysterious land. They were going to a place that until now they had only heard or read about. Their destination was a small town called Odawara on the coast of Sagami Bay, approximately two hours from Tokyo. Since Odawara was a gateway to the Hakone resort zone, Grandfather had built a house there that he sometimes used as a retreat.

Miraculously, Odawara had been spared. It was like the borderline between heaven and hell. Grandfather's magnificent home overlooking Tokyo had been destroyed by the firebombing. Despite the Allies later claims that they were only trying to bomb the industrial part of the city, the large homes exposed on top of the hill s were impossible-to-resist targets.

They arrived in Tokyo on January 13, 1947, about sixteen months after the American occupation began. It was commonly referred to as "MacArthur's Japan." The cool but sunny day made the devastation seem even more frightening. There were hardly any buildings that had remained standing. However, the few structures that survived the bombardments were nothing more than hollow skeletons. The bright sun pouring through the missing roofs made them appear to irradiate from within. Sam remembered Billy saying, "That eerie glow gives me the creeps."

At one point Billy grabbed Sam's arm to bring his attention to a row of buildings. He exclaimed in amazement, "Sam, look at those buildings. You can see right through them." The openings that once were windows became portals through which one could see the next building behind and the next. On and on, it seemed to continue endlessly, empty skeletons of what apparently had been a row of office buildings glistening hauntingly from within.

Billy was visually upset. After searching his thoughts for a few minutes, he asked remorsefully, "Sam, what is this? Why have we come here? There's nothing left."

Sam hardly heard his brother as his own mind tried to cope with the enormity of the devastation.

They made their way to the train station, which was a makeshift structure hastily built with whatever materials could be scrounged together. There seemed to be at least a thousand people milling around, mostly Chinese and Koreans, who were brought to Japan from occupational territories to work as forced laborers. Liberated by the

Americans, they were refugees trying to return to their homelands. Sam and his family eventually settled in among the multitude of confused Asians.

A deep feeling of emptiness came over Sam's body as the reality of the pilgrimage began to strike home. He felt as though he had lost his American identity and become part of the defeated Japanese people. They were all refugees. Mother and Father were returning after being away for over twenty-five years, with every landmark they remembered gone. They had all become part of the wandering mass of humanity.

One of the first signs of recovery from the war were the trains, which were now running. However, each one that arrived was so terribly overcrowded, it was impossible to board. They were forced to spend the night at the crowded station, sleeping on tatami mats, which they had taken with them from the ship. As they rested on the floor, buried among the throng, Billy began to reflect on what they were going through and all the rubble and devastation they had already seen.

He soberly lamented to Sam, "I feel like we have all been swallowed by a giant monster and now we are resting in its stomach, waiting to be sent through its intestines."

Thinking to himself, Sam knew that this was Billy's way of describing the uncertainty of their journey ahead. To help make light of a disturbing situation, Sam jokingly replied, "Yeah, maybe we'll give it a good case of indigestion. Now go to sleep!"

When they awoke in the morning, Father's mat was empty. They weren't immediately concerned because they thought he just had awakened earlier and gone to the latrine. The latrine was a considerable distance from their encampment and required waiting in line to get in. They were all surprised when he suddenly appeared from out of nowhere. He was all out of breath as if he had been running hard.

Father exclaimed, "Hurry! Hurry! I have found a car with a driver." Spontaneously they all jumped to their feet. Father said he had a car, but it really wouldn't have made any difference if he said that he had found a pushcart. They were excited at the thought of leaving that mob. Quickly, they picked up as much as they could carry and ran after him.

After about ten minutes of following Father at a quick pace, Mother realized they had forgotten the tatami mats. When no one volunteered to go back and retrieve them, she said, "Who needs them anyway? Tonight we will be in your grandfather's house."

Coming to a sudden stop, Father indicated that they had arrived. Sam looked around for the car as Father motioned for them to get into a distorted semblance of a vehicle on wheels.

Sam blurted out, "I thought you said you found a car. A better description would have been that you dug up a car."

It had obviously been hit by a bomb. With no spare parts available, it was left in its wrecked condition. However, they all managed to get in as Father proceeded to remind them how lucky they were to have found it. He happened to be absolutely correct. With the scarcity of fuel and most of the road still broken up from all the bombing, cars were expensive to maintain. Even the wrecks were hard to come by.

The route they took to Odawara also took them in the direction of Grandfather's old house. At the last moment, Father asked the driver to make a detour. He explained to Billy and Sam, "I know that I have told you about your grandfather's magnificent home many times. My dream was that someday my children and grandchildren would be able to visit and enjoy its mystical pleasures as I once did.

Unfortunately, according to your grandfather, it has been seriously damaged." In a sorrowful tone of voice, he looked at his two sons and said, "However, it's only a few miles from here and I would like to show you the view."

The road leading to Grandfather's house took them by many homes that were totally destroyed. While Father pointed out the ones that belonged to his friends, Sam could hear the anguish building up in his voice. They could see from what was left that some of the structures had been magnificent ancestral dwellings rich in Japanese tradition. As they arrived at the site where Grandfather's house was located, both Mother and Father were obviously traumatized. Grandfather's home had been completely destroyed. There was nothing left of what was once a majestic structure. An ancient ancestral residence, which had represented their roots and had housed many lifetimes of cherished memories, was gone forever.

Billy and Sam tried to comfort their parents, but they could see the overwhelming horror in their eyes as they stared in disbelief at the city below them. Tokyo, a city that had once glittered with excitement and gaiety, was an endless sea of rubble, stretching far beyond the horizon. Grotesquely twisted hulks of buildings were hollowed out as if they had been devoured by some frightful force that had thrown their skeletons back to Earth to rot.

Sam was personally horrified at the amount of destruction. It was beyond the scope of anyone's imagination. He couldn't help feeling that he had contributed to the monstrous catastrophe. Back in the car, they continued their journey. No one spoke. They just sat there in silence, each one immersed in his thoughts. Father, finally breaking the silence, gave the driver some last-minute directions to Grandfather's retreat. By the time they finally arrived, everyone was totally exhausted.

However, their spirits and level of energy were quickly rejuvenated at the sight of Grandfather's sprawling, typically Japanese-style house.

Sam thought, *If this is where Grandfather spent his vacations, I can't begin to envision what the other home overlooking Tokyo was like.*

The estate had all kinds of fruit trees planted around the property, and in the center of it all was a large pond stocked with fish. To Father's delight, it was Meilee, Grandfather's faithful servant, who graciously greeted them at the front door. Once again, he lovingly embraced her in a traditional American greeting. This time she put her arms around him and kissed his cheek, saying, "I am grateful that the gods have allowed us to see each other again."

Meilee had stayed with Grandfather throughout the war years. As Sam was introduced to her, he thought, *She is as beautiful and gracious as Father had descr ibed her.*

Grandfather was overjoyed and became very emotional as he greeted them. It was a wonderful family reunion. Meilee prepared a special dinner for them that was comparable to a feast. Billy and Sam gorged themselves. Their stomachs protruding, they waddled like stuffed pigs.

After dinner, Grandfather led them into a sitting room where they could rest. As they talked about old times, he removed a bottle of sake from a small glass chest. "I have not had need for this for many years, but now I think its usefulness shall return." He poured a glass for each of them to toast the joyous reunion, and then he refilled them, toasting Father's return. Then refilling them once more, he said, "This time I make a special toast to my two grandsons, who will represent the next generation of the Sagarra family!" As their conversation continued, it was obvious that Grandfather had already been making long-term plans for them.

CHAPTER 27

Over the next few months, as they settled in and became acquainted with their new country, one thing became curiously apparent to Sam. The Japanese people seemed to be accepting the American occupation peacefully. When Sam questioned Grandfather about it, he replied, "The answer goes back to ancient times, to the samurai. The great warriors' code was to fight relentlessly to the conclusion but, if defeated, to accept the victor as their new lord and master. It is easy to understand why the American occupation is peaceful and, so far, successful."

Before continuing, he paused to pour himself a cup of sake. Grandfather still loved his "therapy." He explained further, "General MacArthur is very shrewd. He is like our emperor, with one extraordinary difference. He has accomplished what no one else has been able to do before: successfully unite all of Japan in order to regain our ability to become a productive and self-reliant nation once again." Grandfather paused to sip his sake and to pour Sam a cup.

Sam sat back to absorb what he had been told. He got the distinct impression that Grandfather was more than satisfied with MacArthur's approach and the progress he was making.

His voice became a little more descriptive as Grandfather continued, "MacArthur has even caused a new constitution to be drafted for our government, a constitution that will serve the people rather than rule them. The general has also broken up the industrial monopolies, known as the 'zaibatsu,' that favored the military takeover of the government and supported the war."

Sam remembered Father describing how Grandfather's face would ignite with enthusiasm when he talked about some new project that interested him. He was a great speaker, who electrified and inspired his audiences. In this particular case, it was Sam. He was Grandfather's audience, and he felt the excitement emanating from the conviction in Grandfather's voice.

"MacArthur is determined that Japan will not be taken over by America or any other foreign industrial power. He will make sure that it doesn't happen."

Sam felt Grandfather firmly believed that without MacArthur's relentless determination to keep Japan independent, it never would have stood a chance. To him and millions of others, Grandfather was one of many industrialists who were ostracized and exiled, along with most of the other consortium members, for not supporting the military government's war effort. Sam began to realize that his old grandfather had not been sitting around deteriorating for all these years. A good portion of the membership of his original group was gone, either killed during the war or dead due to natural causes. However, there were enough of them left, and Grandfather had brilliantly kept them together. Crouching back in the shadows like shrewd, experienced old panthers, they stalked their prey and waited for the opportune moment to strike. That moment had arrived!

MacArthur's purge of wartime leaders in the business community removed the top executives of 250 concerns. Although changes had taken place in Japan's industrial world, the large Japanese banks remained intact. Grandfather' s honorable reputation had not been forgotten. It was time to strike, and there was no turning back. MacArthur charted the democracy, and a new constitution was firmly in place. Grandfather and his consortium were back in business, sponsored financially by the Japanese banks. They adopted a new name to signify a new start, and the Nasuco Corporation was born.

Methodically, they started their slow crawl, firing up old companies and, through the fifties and sixties, starting up new ones. Father became a valuable asset to the consortium. With the experience he had in advanced engine technology, he was given control of the automotive division. Billy, with his musical training and fine ear for sound, was put in charge of research and development of hi-fi, stereos, televisions, and other electronic sound equipment.

Grandfather and his consortium had a specific job for Sam. Because of his ability to speak both Japanese and English, he was given control of the acquisition department. He thought about his friend, Commander Harlan Cooper. *Here I go again—another special assignment.*

This time Sam's role was reversed. He would be on a reconnaissance mission for Japan, intelligently "spying" on American manufacturers. His job was to find products that had potential. These products would be brought back to Japan to be improved and reproduced. The Japanese manufacturers eventually became experts at this innovative revamping, and the end result was exporting back to America a far superior product that cost less than if the Americans were to make it themselves.

By 1962 the consortium was well on its way. With twelve successful major acquisitions under its belt and being a majority stockholder in ten other companies, Nasuco was quickly becoming a force to be reckoned with. However, the market that still eluded them was the American automobile market. Sam's father wanted to give it one more shot. Ironically, at the next meeting on January 13, 1963, he stood before the board making the same request he had made almost thirty years earlier. Once again, Father wanted to tackle the American automobile market. He had the support of the younger members of the consortium, who had replaced the older, deceased family members.

Father was much older than they were, but his mind was still alive with visionary ideas, and that's exactly what they needed. Somehow, after all he had been through, he still had his own special brand of tenacity reinforced by Mother's strong determination to keep them together and go on with their lives!

In preparation for the meeting, Father took the precaution of ordering one hundred bottles of sake. Sadly, he could not supply the other missing items—Grandfather's palatial home and his lovely geisha girls. A good port ion of the old guard, along with Grandfather, were still on the board. Exactly as it happened three decades ago, they didn't waste any time attacking his proposal. Leading the assault was Kiyoshi Masuda, now much older and a little heavier but still as cantankerous as ever. In a sarcastic voice, he said, "We have tried this before and failed. It was a very expensive lesson. If we have learned anything at all from this experience, it's that the Americans do not want our small cars. They joke about maybe buying one to keep as a spare in the trunks of their behemoths. *No!* I do not believe they are ready for us yet."

Father felt as though history was repeating itself. He had been in exactly this same position before. Once again he would have to fight for what he believed in. With one very large exception, this time he didn't even have Grandfather on his side.

Father cleared his throat and slowly started to speak. "There are important factors in our favor. The years I spent in America were not wasted. The wealth of technical knowledge gained is irreplaceable, coupled with the new technology that the United States is making available for Japan to use. I firmly believe that Nasuco can produce a superior automobile, a finely crafted precision automobile with such a high degree of dependability and efficiency that it will not deteriorate and break down as quickly as the typical American gas-guzzling behemoth. Nasuco will make a little opening and, as the quality car proves itself, that opening will widen and provide us with the market we have been trying to capture all these years."

Father sat down and silence filled the room. Grandfather slowly rose to his feet and asked the board to vote. Once again, and for only the second time in the consortium's history, Father received a unanimous affirmative vote. He received the board's approval to go ahead. The next step would be to design an automobile that could fulfill all these high standards.

CHAPTER 28

WITH THE AUTOMOBILE BUSINESS moving forward, Sam's job was to find the outlets and distributors that would help set up Japanese dealerships throughout the United States. As the car's final design was completed and production was ready to commence, Sam visited an automobile show in California. His main purpose in attending the exhibition was to recruit individuals to set up distributorships, dividing the country into four sections—east, west, north, and south. It was September 12, 1963, and the turnout for the show was extremely heavy. People had come from all over the country to see the new cars.

Sam had a small booth off the main promenade. Not having a demonstration model, he displayed pictures of the new car on the front walls of the booth. A few people stopped by for information. Besides promoting a good product, Father's company was offering great incentives—incentives that were not available from the well-established American automobile manufacturers. Most of the people Sam interviewed displayed a great deal of interest. It had been a long, hard day's work, and Sam was starting to feel drained.

Just as he was getting ready to dismantle his displays for the night and leave, a couple appeared in front of him, blocking his exit as they stopped to look at the pictures. Sam couldn't help staring at the woman. She was absolutely stunning. Her thick, wavy black hair rolled gently over her shoulders. Milky-white skin with naturally red full lips commanded his attention. However, what attracted him the most were her large, luminous eyes. They were a deep midnight blue, so dark they reminded him of a clear, crisp evening sky. Her lashes were long and gently curved upward, framing those gorgeous, slightly slanted eyes. Sam and the stunning woman just stood and stared at each other. Finally the guy she was with broke the silence, asking for more information on the cars. Sam didn't even hear him. Mesmerized, he thought, *I'm in love!*

Suddenly, snapping out of his semihypnotic trance, Sam tried to concentrate on what the man was saying. His mind kept wandering back to the lovely lady in front of him. *I'm falling in love with a woman*, he thought, *and her husband is badgering me with questions about my cars.* Sam finally turned to look at the man and froze in amazement. The stranger broke the silence first.

"Sam? Sam Sagarra? Is it really you?"

Sam just stood there like a fool. It was a double shock. He still couldn't speak. He was overtired, and his mind had trouble coping with the situation— meeting an old friend whom he hadn't seen for almost twenty years, and falling in love with his wife at the same time. The woman, until that moment, he had never seen before, and he had been literally undressing her and making love to her with his eyes.

Embarrassed and astonished, Sam eventually managed to reply, "Louie? Louie Yoshimo?"

His combat buddy yelled back, "I can't believe it! After all these years, what are you doing here?"

Sam, still not completely recovered from his indecent behavior and shameful intrusion of the beautiful woman's privacy, must have sounded like a fool when he answered Louie in a mortified and confused voice. "I'm trying to sell cars, I mean, trying to recruit distributors."

Louie asked, "Distributors for what? What kind of cars are you selling?"

Sam replied, "Small, high-quality compact cars." For the first time he utilized the new term "compact."

Louie picked up on it quickly. "Compact, I like the sound of that. From these pictures, they look damn good. What are they really like?"

"The pictures really don't do them justice," Sam said. He related just how much time and advanced technology was put into the car's development and how their ultimate goal was for it to be the best of its kind.

Louie became very interested in the whole concept.

When Sam continued with his sales pitch, Louie interrupted, "Wait a minute. Slow down! We have twenty years to talk about. Let's go someplace where we can relax and be comfortable."

Sam thought that was a great idea. He was still dizzy from the whole encounter. Louie suggested that they go for dinner at a small restaurant he had noticed on the way in.

Closing up his booth hurriedly, Sam followed them as they made their way through the promenade to the restaurant on the ground floor. As the waiter led them to their table, Sam felt the need for a moment of privacy and excused himself to go wash up. Louie thought that was a good idea and said he'd join him. Asking Christine, which was the lovely woman's name, to excuse him as well, he told her they would all meet at the table.

When they were finally alone, Sam told Louie that his wife was a beautiful woman. Sam was shocked and embarrassed at Louie's mocking reply.

"Yeah, I noticed that you couldn't take your eyes off her! If she was my wife, I wouldn't have come in here to wash my hands. I'd have them around your throat, choking you to death! This is our lucky day, Sam. After all these years, I travel across the country and meet you, and you come all the way from Japan to meet my sister. This has to be a good omen!"

Sam felt as though he had been resurrected. Suddenly his fatigue was gone and he was full of adrenaline. He laughingly shouted at Louie, "Why didn't you tell me you had such a beautiful sister twenty years ago?"

Louie replied, "Sam, twenty years ago, we had about one hundred thousand Japanese shooting at us from the front and ten thousand Americans trying to shoot our heads off from our left and right flanks, while another ten thousand of our guys, who had just landed and were coming up behind us, were shooting up our ass. If you remember, Sam, it seemed as though the six of us were the enemy. Everyone was trying to kill us." Jokingly, he continued, "I was going to tell you about my sister, but it just slipped my mind!"

Sam grabbed him around the neck as he laughed uncontrollably. At the same time, he pushed him out of the men's room door. After taking a few steps, Sam suddenly grabbed him again by the back of his jacket.

"What is it now?" Louie asked.

Sam nervously inquired, "Is she married?"

Lou ie replied, "No. She's a doctor and never had the time to get serious."

Sam, once again, was relieved and said, "Thank you, God" as he looked upward.

Louie impatiently asked, "Can we go and eat now?"

When they returned to the table, Christine was already seated. The waiter arrived just as the two men sat down. Taking their drink orders, he said he would return with the menus. Sam tried to avoid staring at Christine and concentrate on Louie. He asked him, "What are you doing here at the auto show?"

Louie must have replied, but Sam didn't hear him. No matter how hard he tried, his eyes kept coming back to her. He finally felt that he had to apologize. Addressing Christine, he stammered, "Please, please forgive me for staring, but Louie never told me he had such a beautiful sister."

She blushed slightly. As she picked up her drink and graciously held it up, she said, "Well then, let's make it official. I'm Christine Yoshimo, and I'm pleased to meet you, Sam Sagarra."

The three of them laughed and clinked their glasses together, toasting the occasion. As Louie added, "This is really a miracle," they all took a long sip of their drinks.

When they had settled back in the padded seats, Christine inquired, "Now, let's get back to what were you saying about small, compact cars."

Sam took a deep, thoughtful breath as he prepared to explain. He told them about his father's endeavors years ago to design and build engines for American cars in America and how the war had put an end to that. He continued with a brief synopsis of the past twenty years, encompassing all they had gone through and their eventual decision to return to Japan. He told them all about Grandfather's consortium and MacArthur's miraculous reconstruction of the battle-torn country, and brought them up to date about the birth of the Nasuco Corporation and the tremendous strides they had already made.

Stopping long enough to sip his drink, Sam looked at Louie and said with determination, "This is only the beginning!"

Sam sat back and relaxed, sipping his drink. Christine and Louie remained silent for a few moments as though they were trying to absorb a drama that had just been portrayed on television.

Louie spoke first. "That's one hell of a story, Sam. I would really like to become part of it."

Sam inquired, "How long have you been in the auto business?"

Louie replied, "Since the end of the war. I got a job as a salesman with one of the local dealers in New York. In the early fifties, my brother and I put everything we had into a dealership of our own. Sales were great so we started six more branches, including one each in Connecticut, Pennsylvania, and Delaware. The past ten years have been very good to us."

Ending with a happy statement, he added, "I came out to California to meet my sister and visit the auto exposition, which was topped off by finding an old special friend." Louie picked up his drink up as if to make a toast. "What could be better than that?"

Sam was pleased with Louie's enthusiasm and apparent success. Even more meaningful, he felt that Louie had retained his warmth and down-to-earth personality. Sam always had a special feeling for him and not only because of what they had been through together. He never forgot that hospital visit when Louie had described the death of Danny Kusumo and the enemy soldier, holding hands like brothers on their way to heaven. With emotional tears welling up in his eyes, Louie poured his heart out to Sam about the lovely girl committing suicide when she jumped off the cliff. Therefore, when

Louie asked to be included, Sam knew he had the right man for the job.

Suggesting that they get together the following day to discuss details, Sam turned his full attention to Christine. "Well, now that we all know what Louie and I do, tell me about yourself."

Christine was the type of girl who came right to the point. When Sam asked her about herself, she replied, "Okay." It seemed that, knowing her turn was next, she had a biographical speech all prepared. She carefully recounted, "I grew up here in California. My father is Japanese, and my mother is of Scottish-American descent. While you guys were off fighting the war, I stayed here in California with my Scottish grandparents and finished my schooling. My mother accompanied my father to a concentration camp somewhere in the middle of the desert in Utah. I went to medical school after the war, and my specialty is biochemical genetics." Raising her arms to pantomime a bow, she finished with a flourish. "And here I am!"

Sam was a little surprised but pleased at her straightforwardness. In fact, he admired that. He never liked to beat around the bush or waste time either. He had asked a pertinent question, and she had replied, giving it to him straight and in high gear. Sam thought of leaving well enough alone, but one thing puzzled him and he had to ask, "What is biochemical genetics?" He had no idea what she was referring to.

Christine explained, "Sam, it's an extremely new approach that science is taking. It could eventually change the world of medicine. We believe that many diseases and disorders are genetically transmitted through our sex cells. Researchers analyzing these cells have discovered that they are made up of chromosomes. Breaking them down, scientists have found that each chromosome contains several genes.

"One of the great achievements of the century was the removal of a gene from a living cell. This opened up a new frontier for the world of medicine with the creation of new genetically engineered wonder drugs. These new drugs will eradicate many of the diseases that have plagued mankind since the beginning of time. The company that I work for, Tasco, is at the forefront of genetically engineered gene therapy."

Christine hesitated for a moment to gather her thoughts before continuing, "In the early fifties, scientists discovered that the material the gene is made of, its DNA, serves as the physical basis of heredity, good and bad. That is where I come in. In the future, as we learn more about the gene's basic makeup, we might be able to switch off the bad ones and enhance the good ones.

"Genetic engineering will eventually enable us to actually remove a deformed or mutated gene and replace it with a new one. We might even get to the point someday where we could rearrange the DNA of a gene, creating an entirely new form of life."

As Sam listened to Christine, he became more and more interested. She spoke about her research with such conviction and enthusiasm. She inspired him as well. He interrupted her only for a moment to remark, "How interesting your work sounds. How wonderful it would be if they were to succeed."

Christine replied, "It's great, Sam. I love my work. Sometimes I feel like I'm in a spaceship, somewhere out there in the universe, with each new discovery just beyond the next star."

As she paused, Sam asked her, "Where is this amazing research going on?"

Christine replied, "At Tasco, a fairly new scientific research group, whose headquarters are in Seattle, Washington. I'm working with some of the top biological researchers in the country. They have brought us to the threshold of some revolutionary discoveries, and I'm lucky to be part of it."

Sam inquired, "So you're not living here in California?"

Christine answered, "No. I just came to spend a few days with my brother. We hadn't seen each other for so long that I almost forgot what he looks like."

Seeing an opening to sneak in a compliment, Sam jokingly replied, "Even though your brother has a bad memory"—Louie smiled as he knew Sam was referring to his "It just slipped my mind" excuse—"I'm sure it would be impossible for Louie to ever forget how beautiful his sister is."

Christine blushed and smiled.

Sam, looking at his watch, said, "It's been great being with the two of you. Up until this evening, my stay here has been very boring." He suggested that he and Louie get together the following day.

Louie thought it was a great idea and inquired, "What time did you have in mind?"

Sam replied, "Let's make it after lunch."

Louie asked, "How about the morning?"

Sam, looking directly at Christine, replied, "I don't think so. I'll be busy in the morning. I'm going to start the day having breakfast with a beautiful lady." Still looking deep into Christine's incredible blue eyes, he asked politely, "If that's okay with the lady."

Christine smiled and said, "It's okay with the lady."

Sam excitedly replied, "Great, I'll meet you back here at sunrise."

She replied, "No! That's not okay with the lady. Eight o'clock would be fine."

Sam happily agreed, and the three of them left the restaurant after saying good night. Excitement and warmth filled Sam's body. He also had a feeling of love and tenderness he thought he'd never experience again.

CHAPTER 29

FILLED WITH THE ANTICIPATION of meeting Christine in the morning, Sam didn't get much sleep. The night seemed to take forever to end. He was out of bed at sunrise. After showering and shaving, he dressed and was ready to go. However, it was still only six o'clock and the restaurant was not open yet. He paced in his room for an hour or so until it became unbearable. It was now 7:15 a.m. Not being able to stand it any longer, he left his room. Thinking he would find something to occupy his mind in the lobby, he waited for the time to pass. At seven thirty, the restaurant opened its doors and Sam was the first one in. As the waitress said good morning, Sam requested a table by the fountain. She seated him and brought him a small pot of coffee. Pouring himself a cup, he settled back in his seat to wait for Christine.

Punctually, at eight o'clock she arrived, and he noticed her immediately.

She was wearing a tight-fitting white dress that followed the exquisite shape of her body. It was cut short, just above the knees, which accentuated her long, shapely legs. White high-heeled shoes matched her dress and completed the outfit perfectly. Her long, wavy black hair bounced rhythmically with every step she took as she walked toward him. Sam thought he really must have been tired last night. He remembered Christine being beautiful, but he had been mistaken. She was more than beautiful; she was a goddess.

As she sat down, Sam was at a loss for words other than a gracious good morning and remarking about how wonderful she looked. His mind, once again, went blank as he gazed in amorous delight at Christine.

She asked, "What are we having for breakfast?"

Sam quickly replied, "You go ahead and order. I already see what I want."

When the waitress arrived, Christine ordered her usual juice, coffee, and a small stack of pancakes. Sam requested only another pot of coffee. After not getting much sleep the night before, he found it extremely beneficial in keeping him awake. The waitress soon returned with the order. As Christine drank her juice and started on her pancakes, Sam refilled his cup with coffee. Not saying anything for a while, he remained engrossed with her every movement.

Christine finally remarked jokingly, "You know, you remind me of my father."

Sam was curious. "I do?"

She said, "Yes. When I was a little girl, I was always in some kind of a hurry. I never had time to finish my meals. Every once in a while he would get angry. He would sit down opposite me and tap his fingers until I finished everything on my plate."

Sam laughingly complimented her. "Well, it obviously worked! You filled out in all the right places."

Christine burst into laughter, almost drowning in her coffee. As she regained her composure, she replied, "That's great, Sam. Funny, I never looked at it quite that way."

When they were ready to leave, Sam requested that Christine accompany him when he went to meet Louie. However, she declined.

"You guys have to talk about business, and besides, I would like to do some shopping before I return to Seattle."

Sam then asked, "How about dinner?"

She thought that would be a good idea. She suggested a little place she knew of that had good food and a nice band to dance to afterward. After giving him the address, she said, "I'll meet you there at seven."

The promenade was only one flight up. Looking at his watch, he realized how late it was. People were already browsing. He decided to take the stairs instead of waiting for the elevator. His booth should have been open an hour ago.

Louie arrived right after lunch, and he immediately asked Sam how his breakfast with Christine went.

Sam replied, "Louie, it was great, really great!"

Louie, looking at Sam inquisitively, said, "Sam, it was only breakfast."

Sam replied, "It was more than that, Louie." Stopping for a moment to reflect before his next sentence, he continued, "I want to take her back to Japan with me."

Louie looked at him in silent astonishment before finally snapping back at him, "Did you ask her?"

"No."

Louie exclaimed, "No! No? What do you think she is? A car? Just like that, huh, you decided that you're going to take her back. I don't think it's going to be that easy, Sam. She's really wrapped up in that research project they're working on up there in Seattle."

Sam, soberly questioning Louie, asked, "You think she'll turn me down?"

Louie, grasping the chance to be his usual jolly self, replied a bit sarcastically, "I don't see why she should. I mean, after all, you've known each other for"—he paused slightly for emphasis—"over twenty-four hours. I mean, how long are the two of you going to wait? Sam, you're nuts. I think that bullet hit you in the head twenty years ago."

Sam couldn't help laughing at Louie' s humorous sarcasm.

At Sam's suggestion, they changed the subject and got down to business. Continuing where they left off the day before, Sam explained how he wanted to introduce his car to America. He told Louie, "If we had the right people"—he became more positive—"people who would believe in our product, we could put together a real good promotion, an advertising and marketing program, to introduce our new compact car. I'm sure the car will take over and prove itself a winner."

Louie thought for a moment and said, "I got it, Sam. I've got the guys. You remember Mike Sasaki, the guy who climbed the tree with the whole Japanese army shooting at him?"

Sam replied, "Yeah. How could I forget him?"

Louie said, "Well, he's running one of my dealerships in New York. The guy's great. He will be perfect for the job. Harry Masaka, one of the other guys who was with us, is running my operation in Pennsylvania, and Bobby Nakaoma is out here in California selling auto parts. I bumped into him right here at the show two days ago. I'm surprised that he didn't see you." Correcting himself, he added, "I guess I shouldn't be surprised. You're not really out there with all the action. If I wasn't looking for the men's room, I wouldn't have found you either."

Sam chuckled and said, "I know. If you don't have something that's big and shiny, they shove you somewhere in the corner and out of the way. I'm lucky that they didn't put me in the men's room."

Getting serious, Sam said, "Louie, everyone right now believes bigger is better. We'll have to change their way of thinking. Our promotional campaign will have to convince the American public that compact is better. I know we have the product to accomplish that!"

Louie had a few ideas of his own and spoke with conviction. "You know, Sam, I always wanted to get out of New York. I could come to California and open a distributorship out here." Pausing to catch his breath, he added, "You could send the cars from Japan to California, and I'll ship them around the country, starting with a network comprised of our own guys. I think it would really work."

Sam reached out to shake Louie's hand. The two men clasped their hands together tightly, and Sam exclaimed excitedly, "I'm sure that it will work!" As their eyes locked, confirming their determination, both men felt that they had formed a perfect union.

Sam, for the first time in many years, felt as though things were starting to actually come together. The chance miracle meeting with Louie had accomplished just what he intended when he planned his trip to California. His United States distributorship would be put together with people he could trust. Sam felt confident that the new concept would be a great seller. He had accomplished what he set out to do.

CHAPTER 30

Now, Sam thought, *there's Christine.* If he was able to convince her to come back to Japan with him, his life would be complete. Back in his room, Sam changed in a hurry. His meeting with Louie took longer than he had expected. Running out of the hotel in full stride, he hailed a cab. The cab almost ran him down before it stopped. Jumping in, he gave the driver the club's address and said, "Please step on it!"

The driver turned back to look at Sam. With a smirk on his face, he exclaimed, "Step on it? Do you know where this place is? With all this traffic, we'll be lucky if I can get you there by tomorrow morning."

Pangs of anxiety shot through Sam at the thought of being late. Fortunately, the driver was a sympathetic soul. Sensing Sam's urgency and being in love once himself, he took Sam on a ride through the city that would have amazed any driver in the Indianapolis 500.

Arriving at the club only fifteen minutes late, Sam exclaimed, "That was one hell of a ride! I'd like to have your autograph, but I just don't have the time." Thanking him most graciously, he paid the amount on the meter and gave the driver a twenty-dollar tip.

The amazed driver said, "It's your autograph that I'd like to have." The driver thanked him and wished him luck as Sam flung open the door and ran toward the club.

The timing was perfect for Christine had only just arrived. As Sam hurried into the lobby, he noticed that she had just finished checking her coat. He was relieved that he hadn't made her wait. He had enough on his mind to discuss with her without having to start with an apology. She was wearing a short, tight-fitting light blue dress that was interlaced with an Oriental pattern.

Sam walked up to her exclaiming, "You look absolutely stunning!"

She smiled and graciously said, "Thank you, kind sir."

The club was small and quaint, not exactly what Sam had expected. He thought it revealed a quiet and reserved side of Christine that he hadn't seen as yet.

After they were seated, the waiter asked, "Would you care to order a drink?"

Sam replied, "Yes." Looking at Christine for her approval, he inquired, "How about a bottle of wine?"

Christine nodded.

The waiter left to fill the order and Christine asked, "Well, Sam, how did your day go?"

He replied, "It went very well. With your brother's help, I will be able to accomplish exactly what I came here to do."

Just then the waiter returned with the wine, opening the bottle for Sam to taste and give his approval. The waiter proceeded to pour, filling both of their glasses. Sam lifted his glass to toast Christine.

As she lifted hers, he said, "Here's to us." The band began to play "Unforgettable," and Sam commented, "Very appropriate ... in every way."

Christine gave him one of her unconsciously sensual smiles.

They spent the next few hours pleasantly having dinner and dancing between courses. Sam's anxiety level was continually rising. All evening his mind had been trying to assemble the right words to ask her to marry him and return with him to Japan. He waited until after dessert and couldn't hold out any longer.

Refilling her glass with wine and then his, Sam looked seriously into her amazing eyes and finally said, "I have something I want to ask you."

Christine smiled at him and gently said, "Okay."

Sam continued softly, "I want to marry you."

As he waited for some sort of a reply, there was a long period of silence. He was hoping for some response, but there was none immediately coming. Christine had begun to feel the effects of the wine and finally seemed to come back to life.

Sam asked, "Are you okay?"

She repl ied with an inquisitive "Yes?"

"Then what's wrong?" he asked.

"I could have sworn that I heard you ask me to marry you," she said, stunned.

He simply answered, "I did."

Christine exclaimed, "I thought that the wine was affecting me, but it's not. It's you! The wine has gone to your head; either that or you've completely lost your mind!"

"No, neither one. I'm perfectly coherent and I'm serious. I love you and I want to marry you," Sam said sincerely, meaning every word.

Trying to reason with him, Christine replied, "Sam, do you know what you're asking me to do? I'm a doctor —"

He interrupted, "I know and you can be a good doctor in Japan also."

"Sam, don't interrupt. Just listen to me for a moment." She went on to explain, "I've spent the last five years specializing in genetic research. The Tasco group has been very good to me. I'm working with some of the best scientists in the country, possibly the world. My whole life, until now, has been focused around my work."

Sam, trying to convince her, reasoned, "You could continue your work in Japan. There is a great need for doctors with your experience. Genetic researchers have their hands full. You say that you want to unscramble the mysteries of the gene to create different forms of life. Well, you won't be wasting your time; the radiation from two atomic bombs has already done it for you. You'll have a twenty-year head star t."

Sam's argument temporarily left Christine without words. She didn't know quite how to respond. It was all so sudden. First, he asked for her hand in marriage. Then, he bombarded her with a whole stack of ethical reasons for her to follow him to Japan. Marriage was something to be considered, as she also felt the strong attraction between them. She admired his demeanor, spontaneity, and intelligence. However, leaving the country, she thought, was totally impossible!

His sincerity required a response from her that wouldn't hurt his feelings and, at the same time, made her posit ion clear. "Sam, I know just how you feel. Like you, I was born here and grew up in this country. I went through the same shit you did. Despite all the opposition, I encountered from all those racist bigots, I'm an American and I stuck it out! I paid my dues, completed medical school, and became a geneticist. I am accepted as an equal at Tasco, and I'm working with some of the finest minds in the country. I'm finally getting a chance to shove my success up those racist bigots' asses! Now you come along and ask me to forget it, leave it all behind, and follow you back to

Japan." As she leaned back in her chair exhausted, she said, "I'm sorry. I think the wine is finally getting to me. I feel a little dizzy."

Sam realized he had overstepped his bounds and had to do something fast. Feeling slightly repentant, he replied, "I know it's presumptuous of me to expect you to drop everything, marry me, and leave the United States all at the same time." Not being able to keep back a smile, he added, "You don't have to make a dec ision right now. Think about it, and let me know in the morning."

She threw her table napkin at him, and they both burst into laughter.

The next morning Sam opened his booth at the far end of the promenade on time. Louie arrived about an hour later and found him busily arranging some papers on his desk.

"Glad to see that you're finally getting back to some serious work," he quipped. Sam just stared at him in stony silence. "I spoke to Christine this morning." Sam, trying to pretend he was unaffected by Louie's statement, kept shuffling his papers. "Sam, she called me." Becoming a little more persistent, he insisted, "You've got to give her some time!" Louie pulled up a chair in front of Sam's desk, sat down, and said, "She's all mixed up."

Sam finally asked, "Did she tell you what a fool I made of myself?"

"No, she didn't think that you were a fool at all, maybe a little nuts, but not a fool."

Handing Louie a folder, Sam asked him to go through it. "This is my plan for the distribution network. Give me your critique. I'm going back to Tokyo in a few days, and I'd like to leave knowing that I don't have to worry about it anymore."

As Louie flipped through the pages, he suddenly stopped. Sam, noticing his abrupt conclusion, asked, "What's wrong?"

Louie replied sarcastically, "You know, you probably were always an impatient son of a bitch."

Sam asked angrily, "What's that supposed to mean?"

"I guess it goes back to when we were on that island. Instead of sending a message for the lieutenant to come to us, you had to stand up to get his attention, drawing fire down on us from both sides and almost getting yourself killed. Now, almost twenty years later, you meet my sister and, within twenty-four hours, announce you want to marry her, expecting her to leave the life she's made for herself behind and return with you to Japan. Then you hand me this master plan of a distribution network and want my comments immediately, if not sooner, because you have to return to Tokyo in a few days. Sam, you have to slow down, take a deep breath, and give us a little time to catch up with you. Both Christine and I believe in you. I can deal with your impatience. I'm that way myself when I need to get something done.

"Christine, however, is different. She was hung out to dry, Sam. While my brother and I were off fighting in the Marine Corps, our parents were taken away. We never saw them alive again. They said my father died of cholera. My mother went insane and cut her wrists. They sent her home to Christine in a pine box. She's been on her own ever since. She could have shut the book, Sam, but she chose to claw her way through defeat and make something of herself."

Sam listened to Louie's brief description of the past twenty years and slowly started to relate what had transpired with him and his family. "At first, when I decided to accompany my parents back to Japan, it was because I thought I would never see them again. They had tried for almost twenty years, despite all the adversity and opposition, to become good Americans. Relentlessly they waged their battle against hard-core racists while they were trying to set a good example for their children to follow. My sister was raped, and my brother Charlie died for his fellow Americans. They destroyed my father's dreams. Then, to top it all off, he was thrown into a concentration camp to further dishonor and disgrace him. Besides that, I've got this bullet pressing up against my spine that painfully reminds me of the whole fucking mess every day—"

Louie interrupted, "You know, you're not the only one who went through that shit—"

Sam cut him off. "Wait, let me finish. I knew that my father would never return to this country, so I went with them to Japan for personal reasons. Nevertheless, when we got there, Louie, it was unbelievable. The amount of devastation was indescribable. You could look at pictures forever, but you would never get the feeling of what it was like unless you saw it for yourself. The country lay in ruins. Over six hundred thousand civilians were killed—innocent men, women, and children who were just caught up in the insanity of it all. What made it worse was that I felt I had a hand in all that misery. I felt a desperate need to try to help these people rebuild their lives, especially the children. They were the ones who were hurt the most. Burnt, crippled, missing limbs, and horribly mutilated, they were the ones who had to carry the effects of this nightmare with them for the rest of their lives."

Sam, stopping to catch his breath, got up to pour himself a cup of coffee. Louie, needing a break from Sam's browbeating, thought that was a good idea and joined him. As they faced each other, sipping their hot coffee, Sam said, "Louie, if I seem impatient, it's because I am. The kids who have survived have grown up. I just want to make sure they have something to look forward to."

Sam, becoming more reasonable, said, "Louie, for the first twenty-five years of my life, all I seemed to be doing was fighting for an identity.

Now I finally have one. In Japan, where I blend in with the populous, I'm recognized as Sam Sagarra. I have, at last, become somebody. In America, no matter what I accomplished, I'd only be noticed because I was a Jap in a crowd of Caucasians.

Overwhelmed by Sam's deep resentment, Louie sarcastically replied, "Wow! You've really got your nuts twisted! If you keep thinking like that, they'll twist so tight, you'll never be able to walk straight. Then you won't have to worry about being noticed. As you go hobbling along, people will say, 'There goes Sam Sagarra, the guy with the twisted nuts.' Sam, listen to yourself. You sound like the survival of Japan is on your shoulders alone. That's an awful heavy load for one man. You have already come a long way."

Sam somewhat agreed. "I know we have, and we still have a longer way to go. I feel like we have only planted the seeds—"

Louie interrupted, "That's what I mean, Sam. You have to slow down. Digest what has already been accomplished. Give these seeds a chance to grow. Be careful not to shut the doors or you won't have any place to sell the harvest."

"Louie, I feel like I'm running out of time. I'm already over forty."

Louie, starting to chuckle at Sam's "over forty" statement, replied, "What does that mean? In Japan you're looked upon as a young adult. You would never be considered for a political office until you have reached your seventies or eighties. Many elder statesmen haven't come close to accomplishing what you have in such a short time." Holding up the folder Sam had given him, Louie said, "This represents our seeds. You go back to Japan and send me the 'harvest' and I will make sure that it gets distributed."

Both men were exhausted. They had been going at each other all day. None of it was planned. It was spontaneous. They said what had to be said, and they both felt good about it. From the first, each man knew where the other was coming from. Now, more than ever, they respected each other's beliefs. Saying a warm farewell, Louie wishing Sam Godspeed, and Sam promised to call him when he arrived in Tokyo. Closing the booth as soon as Louie departed, Sam hurried back to his room and collapsed on the bed.

CHAPTER 31

SAM HAD JUST BEGUN to close his eyes when there was a knock on the door. Stumbling, he gingerly made his way toward the door. Opening it, he saw Christine. Thinking he was just dreaming, he closed it. Then he quickly opened it again, asking, "Christine, is it really you?"

She replied, "Yes it is. Are you all right?"

"Yes, yes, come in. I had just dozed of f. I really thought I was dreaming. I never expected to see you again! "Correcting himself, he recanted, "I mean, not like this … not here."

Christine, sensing her sudden appearance had caused Sam a temporary inability to concentrate, said, "Relax. Slow down."

Sam looked at her and irritably snapped back. "All day I listened to your brother telling me to slow down! Is that what you came up here for—to tell me to slow down?"

"No, I didn't," she said, hesitating to gather her thoughts. "I came up here to tell you that you have given me a lot to think about and some pretty damn good reasons to return with you to Japan. However, the most important reason for me to follow you back would be because I love you."

As she finished saying this, their hands reached out and touched. Sam pulled her into his arms and held her in a tender embrace. As he gently kissed her, he could feel her trembling slightly. Remembering Louie' s words, Sam realized that this was new to her. She had always avoided getting too involved, never allowing herself to get this close to anyone. Sam could sense the uncertainty in her kiss.

Every fiber of his mind told him to let her go, but his arms wouldn't listen. As he held her, she returned his kiss and tightened her arms around his neck. Running her fingers through his hair, she kissed him again. It was apparent that she wasn't planning on letting him go either. As she became more relaxed, they settled down on the bed. It was obvious that neither one was making any attempt to hold back. As they moved up on the bed to make themselves more comfortable, Sam caressed her.

Looking into her eyes, he gently asked, "Are we sure we want to do this?"

She looked at him, replying, "You've turned my life upside down in three days. It may be hard for you to believe, but I've never done this before. We might as well go for broke. You wouldn't want to take me all the way back to Japan only to realize that you've imported an inferior product."

Sam had to kiss her to shut her up. He had asked another silly question, and she had responded, giving it to him right between the eyes. He loved her straightforwardness, but she had a way of hitting home, referring to herself as possibly an "inferior product."

Sam tried desperately to keep from bursting into laughter. As he kissed her, Christine sensed his restraint and, still full of spunk, pushed him away gently. "I know I don't have much experience, but one thing I do know is that we're both slightly overdressed for this." Sam cracked up completely. Turning on her side, with her back toward him, she said, "When you stop laughing, would you be so kind and help me with my zipper?"

The zipper was very long, the full length of her back. As he undid it, her entire back was exposed from her shoulders all the way down to the cleavage between her buttocks, unveiling the frilly edge of her bikini panties. His hand trembled slightly as he felt her warm, smooth body. He slowly and lovingly caressed her hip and waist, and hesitating for a moment before he unclasped her bra, he finished his ascent up her back.

Holding her luxurious black hair in his hand, he softly kissed her neck and ear. She moaned with pleasure as he slowly kissed a trail down her back to the top of those tiny, frilly bikinis. His hand pushed under the frills and continued around to her stomach where his fingers became tangled in her pubic hairs. He probed deeper until he could feel her juices flowing. His finger rotated in a slow circular motion while her hips moved in response to the sensual caress. He just lay there for a long while, caressing her and inhaling the aroma of her passion.

As he kissed the back of her neck again, he moved his hand back over her abdomen, over her chest, and under her bra. His fingertips, still wet with her juices, began caressing her nipples until they stood out like ripe berries.

Christine, burning with passion, turned to face Sam. Kissing him gently, she sat up and finished undressing. He undressed hurriedly, and they explored each other's bodies, slowly savoring the newness of their love. He thought she was the most sensual woman he had ever seen. He could wait no longer; he entered her gently, lovingly. She was more than ready for him and wrapped her long, shapely legs around him as she experienced the ecstasy of passionate love for the first time.

On her way back to Seattle, Christine decided to temporarily put the whole thing out of her mind. *All I wanted to do was visit my damn brother, and now I'm thinking of leaving the country with a guy I've only know for three days*, she thought. *How do I tell my friends at Tasco? They are going to think that I've lost my mind, and I'm not so sure that they would be wrong.*

CHAPTER 32

On Sam's way back to Tokyo, all he could think of was Christine. He could still smell her sweet aroma, and the taste of her saliva on his lips filled his mind. A slight feeling of guilt overtook him. He felt that he should have been thinking of the distribution network he had set up with Louie, which was a great accomplishment. Instead his mind was filled with thoughts of Christine.

One week after arriving in Seattle, Christine received a letter from Sam. It contained a one-way ticket to Tokyo with an open date, accompanied by a short note.

> Christine,
>
> You're unforgettable in every way.
>
> P.S. If you hurry, there's a small biological research laboratory here looking for someone with your background and experience. They'd welcome you with open arms, and so would I.
>
> Love,
>
> Sam

Sam's note gave Christine the courage she needed to tell her boss, Karl Watson, the founder of Tasco, that she was planning to leave. As she expected, she was besieged with a torrent of questions. Karl didn't want her to leave. Explaining how important she was to the projects they were working on, he asked, "Is there anything wrong?"

Christine reassured him, "Nothing is wrong. It's just that I've finally met someone I can relate to, Karl. He's someone I feel that I can trust and will also have my best interests at heart."

"Who is this guy?" Karl was worried and upset. Christine was an integral part of his laboratory, and he really cared about her.

"He's an industrialist from Japan. I met him at an automobile exposition in California while visiting my brother. He has asked me to marry him and return to Japan with him."

"Just like that? How about Tasco? How about your work?"

"That's just what makes it work, Karl! I can continue working over there. I've given it a lot of thought, and I believe I can be extremely helpful in Japan. We still don't fully understand the aftereffects of radiation. Who knows what kind of mutations will develop? I have to find a purpose for my life."

Before she could go any further, Karl politely cut her off. "Christine, you're a very intelligent girl. I won't review the facts of life with you. Heaven knows you have been through enough. You can probably rewrite the book. I would just like you to know how I feel. You're the brightest biological geneticist on my staff, and I will miss you terribly. However, if you feel that you need something more purposeful, maybe you are doing the right thing. God knows those people will need every miracle He can spare. Sending you there, He'll know they will be in good hands."

Christine tried not to cry, but her efforts were in vain. As her eyes filled, the tears ran down her cheeks profusely. Karl reached out for her hand and held it lightly. She leaned over and kissed him on the cheek, softly thanking him for all his support.

"You don't have to thank me, Christine. You've more than earned your status. Now you're going out into the world, and I believe there's something important out there for you. I also believe that our work is too closely related for our paths not to cross again. God bless you."

As she left Tasco, Christine felt as though she was leaving her family behind, but her spirit perked up when she thought of Sam and of the new challenges in Japan.

One month later, Sam met her at the Tokyo airport. They were married several weeks later in a grand traditional Japanese wedding. Sam felt as though his life was complete. Christian's love had renewed his feeling for life. He attacked his work with revitalized vigor and a forceful determination that would rival men half his age. With his network of auto distribution in place, he now had time to work with his brother Billy to accomplish the same goals in the electronics division. However, this proved to be more challenging.

The diversity of products required a more intricate network for distribution, compared to the automobile distributors, who were planning to set up approximately fifty dealerships, zeroing in on the most populated cities. As demand increased, they would expand throughout the United States but still on a limited basis in order to maintain control. The distribution of the electronic equipment was much more complex. These products could be sold immediately in almost every existing department store in the country.

The American retailer would give them exposure and distribution. All they had to do was provide a superior product. To kick off his promotional campaign, Sam arranged for Billy and his associates to participate in trade shows around the United States. Growing up in America was a distinct advantage that Sam brought to the Nasuco Corporation. He had a cunning genius for selecting products. Everything he brought back from America—TVs, stereos, cameras, toaster ovens, etc.—Nasuco technicians took apart. They revamped, improved, and enhanced each product's individual performance, using the gift of American technology at first. Then, under Sam's relentless insistence that they had to be better to survive, Nasuco engineers made wondrous technological breakthroughs, uninhibited by corporate bureaucracy and adequately funded by the consortium's banks. They took quantum leaps in almost every sector of the technological market, and in most cases, made comparable American products relics of the past overnight.

Christine found her purpose. She joined Toysukibishi, a group of biological researchers, and Sam was right: they did welcome her with open arms. Her associates referred to her as "a gift from heaven." She was so desperately needed. Sam had been right about that too. The horror she saw during her first year alone would have been enough for any normal person's lifetime. Even in her wildest dreams, she could have never imagined it would be so bad. Her background and experience in genetics brought her instant recognition.

Her patients were the survivors of Hiroshima and Nagasaki. There really wasn't much that she could do for the older people, except counsel them about how to proceed with their lives. Many of the children who were exposed to the radiation died of leukemia, or other types of cancerous malignancies, a few years after the bombs were dropped. However, the children who did survive were now young adults and were coming to consult her for a special reason. They were in their early to midtwenties, recently married, and wanted her advice about having children. This had an emotional effect on Christine for she was already six months pregnant. In her condition, it wasn't easy advising someone else not to have children.

Throughout the following year, in an effort to devise a test that could determine the radiation's effects on her patients, she continuously pushed herself to total exhaust ion, taking time out only to give birth to a healthy six-pound, nine-ounce baby girl. The happy couple named the new baby Nancy. Christine would never forget the wild gyrations of her emotions at that time.

She and Sam were naturally overjoyed with the birth of their first child. Nevertheless, she remarked, "Sam, I feel so guilty."

"Christine, darling, why should you feel guilty?" he asked.

"Because I see so many women who want to have babies, Sam, and they're afraid to. They're afraid because the child might be born deformed. Sam, I want to help them have a normal baby like ours." With tears filling her eyes, she said pathetically, "I just feel so helpless."

"Christine, you're doing all that you can. You've been spending days and nights in that laboratory. I hardly get to see you. Now you have to take some time off to rest and take care of our daughter."

"Sam, I can't. I have so much to do."

"I know, sweetheart. But you'll have to let some of your associates fill in for you."

"No! No, Sam, it's not that. I'm sure that they can handle the regular stuff. It's something, in particular, that I've been working on."

"Christine, what can be so important that you can't take some time off?"

"Every day might count, Sam. I believe that I'm on to something important. Some of the women we've been screening are giving birth to children who seem normal in every way. We have been monitoring them continuously, and except for a few, they're all doing well. I've noticed a pattern of rapid growth. It's been slight, but it is happening. I'm sure that it has to be some sort of genetic change that causes it. What we don't know is if it will eventually cause them any harm. That's why my work is so important."

"What difference does it make, Christine, if they're growing a little faster?

"Other than the fact that these children will mature a little earlier than their peer group, probably no other adverse effects will be visable. However, Sam, if I could isolate that gene, it could open up a whole new world of genetics." Christine was visibly affected by the idea.

"Christine, you have been trying to open up a new world for a good part of your life. How about trying to spend some time in this one with Nancy and me?"

She just smiled at him and said, "I will, Sam. I will."

CHAPTER 33

By the end of 1969, the seeds that bore the fruit of Sam's hard labor were beginning to sprout. With Father's method of strict quality control, learned during the time he spent in America, they were able to send cars to the United States that gave the American consumer everything that their promotional campaign had promised. The distribution network that Louie and his Japanese partners set up was running smoothly. It was a slow but steady growth process, and everyone at Nasuco Corporation was more than pleased.

Everything was going along normally until the early seventies when the Arabs cut back on their production of oil. For whatever reason they gave, it didn't matter to Nasuco. Suddenly, as though struck by lightning, its compact cars, with their highly efficient, low-fuel-consuming engines, skyrocketed to popularity. Putting their factories on twenty-four-hour shifts, they managed to more than double their output. However, they still couldn't meet the demand.

The American auto manufacturers seemed to have been caught with their pants down. The large behemoths were still roaming the country. However, as the cost of fuel kept rising, car sales slowed down to a crawl, giving Japan the chance to speed by. Thrust into the American market with such velocity, Japan became the world's second-largest producer of automobiles within a few years.

At a Nasuco board meeting in 1974, Sam's grandfather and father watched with pride as Sam had the honor of presenting the impressive figures. To everyone's surprise, he also spoke of expanding their electronics business into the world of computers. Most of the board seemed slightly reluctant to consider any further expansion, feeling that even bothering to discuss it at all would be a waste of time. However, Sam persisted. "What we have accomplished is a result of our own tenacity and hard work. Producing products that have proved to be far superior than the ones produced by our American competitors is a victory in itself."

The entire board nodded in agreement and started congratulating one another. Sam had to raise his voice to regain their attention. "What I am concerned about is that we have been producing superior products for a long time, without breaking any sales records. I believe the reason for this is the stigma caused by the product being made in Japan, just another form of racism.

"Then by a miracle of fate, brought about by the Arabs, our products suddenly are in high demand. Our products' dependability and superiority are now being taken seriously, especially the cars. The American cartoonists have even removed the slanty headlights when they draw humorous quips about our compact cars.

"Gentlemen, I just want to make sure that when the smoke clears, our products will have the quality to stand on their own. I firmly believe we should be expanding into computers. The world is getting smaller, requiring information to be at our fingertips. Computers are needed now, but they will run the twenty-first century!"

Sam had given the older members of the board something to think about. They had become complacent. They were satisfied with Nasuco's progress and success and were shying away from any new enterprises that they thought were highly speculative investments.

A member of the old guard, Kiyoshi Masuda, asked to be heard. "Sam, many years ago, your father came before the consortium and presented an idea for building engines using American technology. I was extremely critical of that idea because I thought that it was risky and would hurt our own economy. His version of the future was brighter than mine. I have already eaten my own words because I never truly believed that the Americans would eagerly want to buy our products, especially our small cars. Now almost forty years have gone by. Our consortium has survived recessions, a worldwide depression, a catastrophic war, occupation and reconstruction of our country, and finally"—complimenting Sam—"with your guidance, we have successfully rebuilt our industrial might." As Kiyoshi Masuda paused, all of the consortium members rose to their feet, looked at Sam Sagarra, and applauded. However, Masuda wasn't finished.

He continued, "Our automobile factories are working at full capacity. The shipbuilding facilities are producing great tankers and cargo ships for the world market. Our scientific achievements in electronics are in the forefront of the industry, leading the world into the future. The consortium has given birth to Nasuco Corporation. Comparable to a little cub, it has grown and is beginning to roar like a mature lion. We must be careful not to overfeed it, making it too heavy to conquer its next prey. Now you talk about computers. I will support you, but the final decision shall be made by the younger members. They are the ones who will have to face the future, living with the decisions we make today."

Most of the old guard remained skeptical; however, all of the younger members knew that Masuda was right. Supporting Sam Sagarra was an intelligent move. He had already proved himself in every way. He was a shrewd and aggressive leader, who never liked procrastinating, always taking the initiative and making things happen. Besides, many of the younger members knew that Sam already had scores of technological and industrial spies infiltrating major facilities around the world, especially the United States. During private meetings, they had arranged unlimited funding to be provided by the consortium. The younger members had known long before the meeting that the old guard would put the burden of expanding into unfamiliar territory on their shoulders.

Sam was creating his own keiretsu. He wanted to have control of every product they manufactured and each phase of its production. With the consortium's funding, he acquired all of the smaller companies that made components for Nasuco products. Uniting them under one banner gave him the assurance of quality control and on-time delivery. Sam had created a conglomerate that ran like a precision instrument, and as their profits soared into the billions, his control became unquestionable.

CHAPTER 34

On August 5, 1975, Grandfather had a stroke. As his condition worsened, all the members of the family and some of his closest friends assembled at his home. He was a tough old man. Even though he was on his deathbed, he was still chairman of the board and would never allow himself to die without having the last word. Everyone was summoned to his room, and he spoke to them in a low but steady voice. "I have completed a full cycle."

He explained, "I took part in Japan's first industrial revolution during the nineteen twenties, watched her become a mighty military power, and saw her destroyed. Now I am thankful to the gods for letting me live long enough to take part in her reconstruction, experiencing with delight my family's participation in Japan's second and greatest industrial revolution." Pausing, he reached out to hold Sam's hand. Grandfather looked into Sam's eyes and, in a firm voice, exclaimed, "You are Japan's second rising sun!"

Grandfather died peacefully a few hours later. Sam's father followed him in succession but only in status. It was really Sam who became the leader of the consortium, a master of manipulation and diplomacy with billions of dollars at his disposal. He wined and dined any head of state who would help Nasuco increase its exports.

Exactly as Grandfather predicted, Sam laid back like a panther with a heavy cash reserve. His prey became any ailing American company that would benefit Nasuco. His tactics sometimes became ruthless, holding cash over the unsound company's head until it threw in the towel and agreed to his terms. By the mid eighties, Nasuco had either bought or acquired a large portion of stock in American companies, which became a major factor in the health of the US economy.

Finally having his fill of corporate acquisitions, Sam turned his attention to American real estate. With Nasuco's cupboards still filled with a seemingly inexhaustible supply of cash, Sam was like a child let loose in a candy factory. With an insatiable appetite, he virtually inhaled premium real estate all across the United States. While it was considered a good investment, the consortium also looked at it as a safe haven for its hard currency.

As the pace escalated, the American people began to take notice. The general frame of mind was "We don't mind buying Japanese-made products. However, what we do mind is them coming back and buying America with the money we gave them. They will be the landlords, and someday they may decide to evict the tenants."

Prior to the Nasuco Corporation annual board meeting of January 1989, Sam requested the presence of the entire consortium. There were matters of utmost importance that required the full membership. They were going to have to make decisions that could change their present way of doing business.

Sam, by design, was early for the board meeting. He had his coat over his arm as he approached the CEO's secretary. "Good morning,

Shirley. It has been a long time since our last meeting. I hope that you're enjoying your position here at Tasco."

She smiled warmly and shook his hand. "I have taken care of that little task," she said as she handed him a small envelope. Sam quickly placed the envelope in his breast pocket.

She asked Sam if he would like a cup of coffee, but he declined, knowing that breakfast would be catered in the boardroom that morning. Shirley was his protégé. He primed her and secretly helped her secure his position. For her help, she received a stipend from him every month. She was his mole and nothing that Tasco did was secret from him.

It was a seemingly innocent meeting. She was polite and courteous as a secretary should be to a visiting executive. It was time for him to head to the boardroom, and Shirley guided him there. The room was full of executives preparing for this meeting.

Shirley led him to his chair and said, "Certainly, sir, I'll be glad to watch your luggage for you until the meeting is over."

Sam was to be the main speaker. When he addressed the meeting, he started vocalizing his resentment of American arrogance, thoughts he had suppressed deep inside for years. "The harsh treatment of my family in the United States during the war years has remained imbedded in my mind for decades. I have never directly sought revenge. However, the rise of Nasuco to national prominence has provided me with plenty. The Americans have taught us well, and we were excellent students. After almost forty-five years of playing the game their way, they suddenly want to change the rules because we are winning. Now the ugly head of anti-Japanese sentiment has started to rise again. I believe the Americans are going to declare war, but this time it will be a different kind of conflict.

"They have become a complacent society, a lazy, laid-back nation of consumers." Sam had gained their total attention. The members listened intensely with slight apprehension about where his speech was going to lead them. "*We* are a pragmatic people. We have learned from our mistakes. Filled with national pride, we have tenaciously pushed forward and earned every inch of success we have gained. The Americans sweep their mistakes under the carpet or like an ostrich stick their heads in a hole. They think that if they can't see their mistakes, they'll disappear.

"It has become increasingly apparent that they consider us one of their mistakes," Sam continued. "Unfortunately for them, they don't have a carpet large enough to sweep us under. If they choose to bury their heads in a hole, we will still be there when they believe it's safe to come out.

"Gentlemen, we have become a stark reality." For the first time that anyone could remember, Sam's voice rang with a tone of vindictiveness.

"We are a force they will have to deal with. If the American public's criticism continues, its administration will have to get tough, and we should be prepared to push back."

Sam continued, "This war will be different. It's an industrial war, and we are ahead. Our stiff quality-control procedures, together with many consecutive years of technological breakthroughs, have made our products far superior. The Americans will try to regain the initiative, but they will fail. We are winning without firing a bullet. Gentlemen, our bullet is the outstanding success of Nasuco Corporation. We have accomplished peacefully what couldn't be done by war. We have learned from our mistakes. Unlike Pearl Harbor, where Japan hit and ran, this time we are already on the mainland in every home."

Sam pointed out, "We influence almost every aspect of their daily lives. It will take the Americans many years to catch up to what we have now, and by then, we will be ahead of them again. The cycle may continue indefinitely, making them more agitated and aggressive toward Japan. We should be prepared with counter measures should this occur."

One of the younger members of the board raised his hand to be heard. "I am concerned about the rest of the industrial world. They are all watching to see how we work out our differences with the United States."

Sam replied sarcastically, "Let's finish up with America first. Then we will turn our attention to the rest of the world."

Sam kept the floor and continued, "Gentlemen, let me remind you that so far we are only talking about an industrial and technological war with America. Toysukibishi, our biological research division, has made many miraculous scientific discoveries. We are at the doorstep of a major breakthrough in the world of genetics." Toysukibishi was another one of Sam's "cash-poor" versus "cash-rich" acquisitions. Twenty years ago, when the company was in need of funds to continue, Sam held out his cash in front of them like a carrot and acquired the whole company. He would later say, "It was a birthday present for Christine."

"My wife, Christine, has been the head of the facility for the past ten years. She has informed me that they have been experimenting in areas that the Americans haven't ethically approached. When they realize what direction our research is going in and the marvelous achievements Toysukibishi has already made, another shock wave of anti-Japanese sentiment will engulf their country. Washington will attempt to conceal the fact that we are ahead of them again and try to catch up to us. They will declare war, this time for ethical reasons.

"I have already discussed privately with some of you a few counter measures that I have in mind. We should talk among ourselves and reconvene this meeting in forty-five days to zero in on a defensive plan."

As Sam finished his speech, the members spoke softly among themselves. The older ones didn't like to hear anything referring to war, reminding each other that America had been Japan's only true friend. The younger members, being a little more aggressive, mumbled to each other, "If it's a war America wants, we should be prepared to give them one."

CHAPTER 35

Marcy Watson was hurrying through her daily routine. She still had a million little things to do. The last stop on her way home would be to pick up her new gown. Marcy was a tall, shapely brunette. Although she always was immaculate about herself, she never really cared much for fancy dress. In her daily routine, it really didn't matter what she was wearing. Her clothes were always covered by a laboratory gown. However, whatever she gave up in personal appearance, she more than made up for in her relentless striving for perfection, continuously pushing herself and her constituents to total exhaustion.

Tonight was different. She was going to attend a gala celebration commemorating the golden (fiftieth) anniversary of Tasco, the scientific biological research conglomerate founded by her father and her uncle. What made this evening extra special was the fact that she was going to be honored for her devoted leadership and outstanding achievements in genetics. Scientists from around the world would be there to congratulate her.

After her father died, Marcy succeeded him as chairman of the board at Tasco. A few years ago, when her uncle retired, his son Gene

Watson became president. David Watson, Marcy's nephew, was a vice president, and he was flying in from Tasco's headquarters in Seattle to be with his aunt on this momentous occasion.

David had only recently returned from a trip to Japan, where he had been the guest of the Toysukibishi Research Group. Tasco and Toysukibishi were working on similar projects. David and a few of his associates were invited to discuss a possible joint venture between the two laboratories. However, the excitement fueling David's adrenaline through his veins wasn't only regarding the news he had to report about Toysukibishi. It concerned a girl he had met and fallen in love with in Japan. David had written Marcy about all this before returning home. Knowing his aunt's fiery temper, he had no idea how she would react to the part of the letter where he described his love for Nancy.

David and Marcy had become very close throughout the years, working together on projects that sometimes went beyond the normal boundaries of ethical acceptance. Fortunately, many of these undertakings yielded miraculous breakthroughs in the field of genetics. The work done in their laboratories enabled Tasco to be in the forefront of molecular biological research, devoted primarily to the application of scientifically engineered gene therapy. The drugs they had created carried corrective genes, curing many ailments that had plagued mankind.

Marcy was the queen of Tasco, and David was her knight in shining armor. There were many times at annual board meetings that he had come to her defense over a particularly controversial project. However, she was no pushover; when provoked or challenged, she never backed away from a good fight. Her deep emerald-green eyes would fire up like two burning lasers, and her vicious attacks had cut many an adversary down to size.

What infuriated Marcy the most were the blocks thrown at her for ethical reasons. She was a great believer in humanity. Anything that would make life better was the path for Tasco to follow. Being the only woman on the board, she got a special delight out of threatening to cut the balls off any man who got in her way. Their latest project, however, had become the most controversial of all: the dormant part of the human brain. Their research had unraveled the mysterious portion of the human gene that controlled intelligence. At the present time, the human brain was only being utilized at approximately 10 percent of its capacity. By creating genetically engineered intelligence genes that could activate the other 90 percent, the realm of human accomplishment would be unlimited. Despite the objection of almost all of the members on Tasco's board, she and David went ahead with the controversial research.

For their experiments they had selected a female chimpanzee named Margo, who had already displayed an unusually high degree of brilliance on her own. Margo was a very gentle animal, not prone to the mischievous, spontaneously clowning behavior normally associated with the species. She seemed to have the ability to concentrate, sort of analyzing each move she made. Believing that she would also make a good mother, Marcy and David selected her for their new project.

They artificially implanted a fertilized egg, whose original genes had been altered to reflect and enhance the animal's intelligence. The major objective of the experiment would be to see how much, if any, of the unused portion of the offspring's brain would be activated. After a normal gestation period, Margo presented them with a healthy baby male chimp. He was cute and slightly larger than other chimps at birth.

Within a few weeks, he was waddling around and trying to sit erect, but he kept rolling over onto his back. However, he wouldn't give up; he was determined to master the difficult task. Over and over again, he persisted. With each attempt, his chattering became louder, filled with frustration. The baby was so hilarious that they named him Chico. It just seemed to fit.

A normal chimpanzee's intelligence and ability to learn, within its first two years, accelerates at approximately twice the rate of a human baby of comparable age. After that, it begins to slow down and eventually comes to a crawl. Chico's schooling started almost immediately. By the time he was six months old, he was able to differentiate between colors. They set up three boxes, red, green, and yel low. When he pushed the button on the red box, a little door would open displaying a banana, which he would proceed to eat. Upon pushing the green button, he recovered an onion. The yellow box gave him an orange. After biting into his first onion, he never pushed that green button again.

By Chico's first birthday, they had worked out a pattern of sign language, using hand signals that Chico absorbed quickly. Each signal represented a different fruit. When given a particular sign, he could push the proper buttons on a computer to display the corresponding fruit. He developed a passion for the computer. Chico knew it was his method of communication. He loved to press the keys. As he got older, they intensified his lessons. David and Marcy set up the computer to display Morse code with beeps and buzzes so he could relate to the dots and dashes. Within two months, Chico was able to remember the proper combinations of dots and dashes to reward himself with ten different treats. Except for being able to speak, there seemed to be no limit to his ability to learn.

On his first birthday, David and Marcy presented Chico, all dressed up in a little black tux and bow tie, to a joint meeting of the National Board of Biological Research and the National Board of Ethics. Chico didn't let them down. He went through his array of accomplishments without a hitch. Everyone unanimously agreed that he had an exceptionally high level of intelligence, and they were amazed at the depth of his retention.

While applauding their success, they were quick to caution Tasco to limit their experimentation to chimpanzees, making it very clear that they were not ready to sanction any testing on human beings. To Marcy and David, however, it was more important that their hard work all these years had paid off. Chico represented a major scientific breakthrough in genetically activating the dormant portion of the brain. They had discovered an entirely new world, a new frontier of unlimited intellectual capability.

After the meeting, they knew that going forward would be slow, but nevertheless, they were on their way into the future with refueled enthusiasm. They were confident that the discovery made by the Tasco Research Group would be used for the betterment of mankind.

CHAPTER 36

DAVID'S EXCITEMENT MADE IT impossible for him to relax. Unable to stay in his room any longer, he decided to go down to the hotel lobby and await his aunt's arrival. He could hear the music coming from the ballroom, where they were preparing to greet her. When her car finally arrived, David ran past the bell captain. Beating him to the door, he graciously opened it for her. As she got out, he bowed and said, "Welcome, your majesty."

He had always kidded with her. Knowing his aunt so well, he was aware that this wasn't her thing and she would be very nervous. Marcy loved him for trying to help calm her nerves.

Laughing with a devilish look in her eyes, she said, "Okay, okay, you clown, that's enough! Now tell me about Nancy." Marcy, knowing her nephew so well, felt that Nancy would be foremost in his mind. Placing her arm through his so he could formally escort her to the ballroom, she asked once again persistently, "Come on, David, tell me what's she like."

"Marcy, she's wonderful."

"I kind of got that from your letter, but I want to know what she does."

"She's a biochemical geneticist. She joined her mother at Toysukibishi a year ago."

Marcy asked, "She joined her mother?"

David replied, "Yes, her mother is Christine Sagarra. She has been head of the facility for years."

"So, you want to marry the boss's daughter? What's her mother like?"

"She's a remarkable woman, Marcy. She was born here in America. After a rough childhood, she worked her way through college, becoming the leader in biological research. In fact, her first position was with Tasco."

Marcy replied, "I know! I remember my father talking about a bright and promising biologist and how disappointed he was when she decided to leave. I came on board a few years later, and my father was still talking about Christine. I would like to meet her someday. Anyone who could impress my father the way she did must be one hell of a researcher. Now let's hurry along. We'll continue this conversation later."

They arrived at the ball room, and as they entered, David could feel Marcy's arm tighten around his. When they were noticed, the entire ballroom erupted into applause. Marcy tightened her grip on David's arm. Just in case he had any idea of setting her free, he could forget it. She could be a tough, ass-kicking bitch, when the pressure was on, but usually she was a shy person, avoiding this type of affair. She had spent her whole life working alongside her father at Tasco, taking over the reign when he died. The facility consumed her. However, this particular award presentation was one that she couldn't be excused from because she was the guest of honor. She was wined and dined and held up for all the world to see. After a few congratulatory speeches, Marcy was presented with a plaque, commemorating the many years of research that she and her father had devoted to the advancement of mankind.

Marcy was overwhelmed with gratitude, not so much for herself but for her father. It was his high standards and tenacity that she had inherited. Everything she had accomplished she felt was due in part to him. When the ball finally ended, she was thankful that it was Friday evening and she would have the weekend to recuperate.

David, eager to continue his conversation, arrived early on Monday morning, but he wasn't the first one there. As he abruptly entered the laboratory, he startled Marcy, who had been peering into a microscope. Surprised to see her at work so early, he said, "My God, didn't you go home? I'll bet you came here right after the ball and worked right through the weekend. You know, one of these days, your nose will disappear and you'll have this microscope hanging there in its place."

Marcy broke up, laughing uncontrollably. "Okay, okay, you win. I'll take a break. Let's go into my office. We'll be comfortable, and you can finish filling me in on your visit to Toysukibishi."

As they entered her office, David smelled the aroma of a fresh pot of coffee perking. "Ah! We arrived just in time. I haven't had breakfast yet."

Marcy said, "Good, you pour the coffee and I'll get the chocolate chip cookies."

Now David really knew that he was with his aunt Marcy. They had both been chocolate chip cookie fiends for years. After practically inhaling a dozen cookies, they looked at each other and giggled.

With her last cookie gone, she smiled and said, "Enough with these damn cookies. Now tell me about your trip."

David, taking time to gather his thoughts, finally said, "Marcy, I don't know where to start." Slowly he began to relate an unbelievable tale. "Christine and her associates at Toysukibishi started many years ago. While trying to help young pregnant women who had been exposed to the radiation of the atomic bombs, they observed that a small percentage of the babies born displayed a very slight pattern of rapid growth. Working with these children, they were fortunate enough to isolate this hybrid gene. Throughout the years, they successfully implanted the gene into mice, guinea pigs, and rabbits with amazing results, almost doubling the rate of growth in each species. Six years ago, in 1989, they secretly implanted the gene into a human egg fertilized in a test tube. They nurtured the embryo in an incubator and raised it in the laboratory."

Marcy gasped. "My God, David. It sounds like I'm listening to a horror story. I think what you are telling me is that this child was conceived, nurtured in an incubator, and grew up in a laboratory without ever feeling the warmth of a mother's womb. David, it sounds monstrous."

Thinking to herself, she couldn't help chuckling as she recalled her familiar threat "to cut the balls off anyone of the board members who stood in her way." Still laughing, she told David, "If I ever tried to convince the Tasco board to sanction that kind of experimentation, I'd have twenty-four sets of balls to bronze."

Marcy became more serious. "David, do you remember the tough time the board of ethics gave us over Chico? They would rip us apart on something like this. Okay, so now tell me what they want from us."

David said, "Toysukibishi wants to do a joint venture."

Amazed, Marcy asked, "A what?"

"They want our intelligence gene."

"What for?"

"Well, they have a problem," David continued. "When they experimented on mice and rabbits, it didn't make much of a difference. They matured quickly, but they had no way of testing their intelligence in relation to their size. Now they have Tamaki, a six-year-old boy with the normal brain capacity of a six-year-old in a body that should belong to a fourteen-year-old."

Unable to think of an immediate response, Marcy remained silent as David finished speaking. She got up for another cup of coffee. Taking another handful of chocolate chip cookies, she laughingly remarked to David, "If I go along with you on this, I will be able to eat as many of these cookies as I want to and not have to worry about my weight. Having you around is real good for my diet."

David smiled and asked, "How come?"

Marcy, with a mouthful of cookie, sprayed David as she yelled back, "How come? I'll tell you how come! When we present this idea of yours to the National Board of Ethics for its approval, the members won't let us leave their office alive. I'd never have to worry about my weight again. That's how come! They might be able to get away with that kind of experimentation in Japan, but this is the United States. Here, if the ethics committee didn't stop us, the church would."

"Marcy, there must be some way we could work in conjunction with them. If we worked together and we were successful, the end result would be mature human beings at the age of sixteen with brains like computers."

Marcy snapped back, "If we were successful? What happens to the failures? Are they considered human beings, or do we just throw them out in the garbage like a wilted plant?" Her voice became more intense and more definite as she reasoned with him. "David, I was conceived through the love of my mother and father and blessed by the hand of God. This Tamaki you are referring to was created in a laboratory by Toysukibishi and blessed by Japan.

"I'm sorry, David, but this whole concept doesn't rest easy with me. Besides, we would need your cousin Gene's approval. Knowing how he feels about what the Japanese consider fair-trade methods, I don't think we could ever get him to go along with something like this. In fact, I'm sure he would never trust them." Marcy finally suggested, "Let's give it a rest for today. I'll see if I can get a hold of Gene, and we'll talk about this again tomorrow."

CHAPTER 37

Gene Watson was a conservative individual but usually outspoken in his beliefs. While trying to keep a lid on Marcy's controversial experiments, Gene spent most of his time at odds with her. Throughout the years, David had become the wedge between them, successfully breaking up many deadlocked situations. However, this time, Marcy knew she would be better off talking to a stubborn, simple-minded jackass, and she was right.

The following day she met with Gene and briefed him on David's trip to Japan, filling him in on Toysukibishi's research, the child Tamaki, and the Japanese progress in molecular genetics. She finished by explaining Toysukibishi's proposal to cooperate in a joint venture, combining Tasco's genetically engineered intelligence gene with its rapid-growth project.

His response was exactly what she expected. "Nuts! Nuts! You are both fuckin' nuts! You want to put our intelligence gene into one of their fuckin' homemade monsters? Marcy, you can play around with the brain as much as your heart desires, and I have to admit, you have made some miraculous discoveries. However, this thing Toysukibishi has made, this child Tamaki, is the manufacturing of life! Marcy, they're interfering with God's work! I shudder at the thought of what we might create. In fact, I can see it all now very clearly. On a dark night, thousands of people carrying torches will be coming to kill the goddamn thing. Marcy, this time I think both you and David have lost your minds!"

For the first time in her life, Marcy was speechless. After Gene's sarcastically graphic reply, she stood there for a moment. Knowing that he was right but not being one to back down from a fight, she fired back with her own little sarcastic put-down. "Sometimes I wonder where you came from. Why don't we let the board decide this one?" Turning, she stormed out of his office, slamming the door behind her.

At Tasco, in order to review and follow the progress of each project, the board met every week. Therefore, Marcy and David didn't have long, so David presented the possibility of participating in an experimental joint venture with Toysukibishi to the board. After relating the details and explaining the parameters of the experiment, he sat down. As he and Mary expected, Gene Watson didn't waste any time. He asked to be heard and came at them with double barrels blazing.

"Gentlemen, after the war, Japan was like a wounded baby dinosaur whose parents had just died. We took the helpless, orphaned little baby and nurtured her on a rich diet of technical knowledge, along with the technicians to hand-feed it. We held her up so she could learn to walk again. As the dinosaur grew, it developed an insatiable appetite for our dollars, and we absorbed its excrements in the form of cars, computers, cameras, TVs, VCRs, and hundreds of other products.

"Now this baby dinosaur has become a fully grown monster, and we, having nothing left to feed her, are beginning to be devoured. In my opinion, we are becoming nothing more than a colony of

Japan. Gentlemen, if we participate with Toysukibishi in this unholy experiment to create monsters, Japan will once again gain control of our technology, and the experiment will come back to haunt us."

David responded quickly, counterattacking Gene's statement. "If anything comes back to haunt us, it will be my cousin's shortsightedness. If we don't participate with Toysukibishi now, while we have the opportunity, we will be left behind again. Eventually their researchers will develop their own intelligence gene while we are bogged down here with our ethical review boards, who so far have only granted us permission to produce intelligent chimpanzees that can slice a banana with a knife and eat their cereal out of a bowl with a spoon. Toysukibishi will be creating human beings with brains a thousand times more sophisticated than any computer in existence. I think it would be a big mistake for Tasco to ignore Toysukibishi's invitation to participate in this joint venture."

Marcy, sensing the tension building between David and Gene, knew she had to do something fast before they exploded. Calling for a recess, she and David left the room. As they walked down the hall toward the lounge, David said, "Wow, I need a drink! That bastard is really getting to me again. Why do we have to put up with his bullshit every time we present a new project?"

Marcy replied, "Come on, David, normally I would agree with you, but this is not just 'another' project. Look, when we go back in there, I'm going to suggest that you take a committee back to Japan, meet with Toysukibishi, and let the committee decide whether or not we go ahead. This one is too big for you and me alone to push down the board's throat."

David agreed with her faultless logic. Besides, it would give him a chance to see Nancy again.

Two weeks later, David and his four-man committee were on a plane to Tokyo. An entourage of Toysukibishi associates, led by Nancy, met them at the airport. The greetings were warm and casual, except for Nancy's. She gave David an old-fashioned American welcome, throwing her arms around his neck and giving him a warm, loving kiss.

The following morning, they got the royal tour of the Toysukibishi facilities. For lunch they were treated to an elegant display of various types of fish at the facility's restaurant. One of the committee members, tasting a piece of fish, remarked how delicious it was. "Was it made here?"

One of the executives jokingly replied, "No, it came from the ocean."

Everyone laughed politely.

As the day went by, the Tasco representatives got a firsthand look at some of Toysukibishi's outstanding research projects. However, as they started zeroing in on their rapid-growth project, David could feel the apprehension in the air. After meeting Tamaki, their feelings were mixed, somewhere between pity and compassion. David's four-man committee was not exactly pleased with the liberties Toysukibishi had taken in totally disregarding the possible failure of their experiment. There was this six-year-old boy stuck in this huge body, psychologically confused and waiting for his mind to catch up with his size, which they all felt would never happen.

His physical growth would always be ahead of his intellectual growth, eventually leaving him mentally disturbed. The committee began arguing among themselves, but they all seemed to agree on one thing: Toysukibishi had gone beyond the normal parameters with Tamaki, far beyond the ethical boundaries they had to adhere to in the

United States. They also felt that Toysuki bishi had an ulterior motive for wanting Tasco's intelligence gene.

The following day, they voiced their valid concerns to David. After trying for an hour to convince them that they were overreacting to the Tamaki experiment, David finally realized his efforts were in vain. They had made their final decision, and they were leaving tomorrow.

Sensing David's disappointment, the spokesman for the group said, "David, we want you to come with us. If we leave without giving them a positive answer, we feel you might be in danger."

David considered his remarks and replied, "If I decide to join you, I will be at the airport in the morning."

Later that day, David met Nancy for dinner. They were in a small, quaint restaurant in the heart of Tokyo. From the moment they were seated, Nancy could see that David was disturbed. As they ate, he hardly spoke at all. Finally, unable to hold back any longer, she asked him, "Is something wrong?"

He replied, "It has been a very frustrating day, and I guess I'm just tired."

"Did something happen at the labs?" she queried.

"Yes," replied David sadly. "I'm afraid so. It's my committee. They are extremely uncomfortable with the Tamaki experiment, and it has completely thrown them out of joint."

As he became more irritated, his voice rose slightly. "The worst part is they feel Toysukibishi has ulterior motives for requesting Tasco's help. They're leaving tomorrow, and they want me to come with them. They believe that if I stay here alone, I could be in danger. Personally, I think they are overreacting. They have been wrapped up in this ethical crap so long, it has finally gone to their heads!" Visually fatigued, he finished his drink in one swallow.

Nancy could feel David's frustration. If she didn't do something, this whole thing could blow up in her face and she would lose him forever. "David, they are not overreacting!" He looked at her inquisitively, as she continued, "There is something wrong, something very wrong, and it's starting to scare me."

As she hesitated, David asked, "Nancy, what is it that's frightening you?"

She looked at him in silence. He could see the fear building in her eyes. He reached out and held her trembling hand. David, becoming very concerned, tried to comfort her. "Look, sweetheart, whatever it is, if you think it's really that bad, maybe we should both get the hell out of here."

As she started to calm down, he became more alert and persistent. "Okay, now tell me what's going on."

She drew back slightly, as though she wasn't sure that she was doing the right thing. She realized that once she revealed her secret to him, his life would really be in danger.

CHAPTER 38

NANCY'S ANXIETY ABOUT THE perilous reality of the entire situation became evident. She had to tell David. Possibly with his help, they could put a stop to this madness. Nancy took a card from her purse and held it out for David to see. "The other day, I received this from the laboratory."

David looked at it for a moment. "Okay, I see it. It's a card with your picture on it, obviously an identification card."

"Yes, it's an ID card with my picture on it, but David, it's not mine." Pointing to the bottom left-hand corner of the card, she said, "You see these numbers? Well, they don't correspond with my original card."

After examining it for a moment, David replied, "Okay, so they made a mistake with the numbers, but your name is on it."

Nancy impatiently said, "David, it's a computer error." Pointing to the opposite corner of the card, she said, "You see these letters, J-D-S? That's not my department."

David, looking at her curiously for a moment, remained silent as he tried to comprehend. "Okay, okay, I hear what you're saying and can see that the card is obviously a mistake, but what does it mean?"

"David, JDS is a group that not too many people know about. The only reason that I do is because I have heard my father speak of them occasionally."

Suddenly picking up her purse, she politely ordered, "David, pay the check and let's get out of here."

More than slightly confused, he obeyed. They left the restaurant, and she led him to her car. Asking him to get in on the passenger side, she slid behind the wheel.

As they left the parking lot, David inquired, "Where are we going?"

Nancy replied, "To the airport."

Taken by surprise, he asked, "What for? I have a morning flight."

She replied, "I'm not taking you there to leave. I want to show you something. Then maybe we will leave together."

When they arrived at the airport, she made a right turn and drove approximately two miles to a closed gate, guarded by two uniformed soldiers carrying automatic weapons.

David, unable to contain his curiosity any longer, said, "Nancy, what the hell is this place?"

"You'll see," she replied as she fumbled through her purse for the I D card. "I tried this once before, when I first received the card, and they let me pass through." David became very concerned as she added, "Maybe it will work again."

"Nancy, what do you mean *maybe* it will work again?"

As they approached the guards, she told him, "Be quiet! Don't ask so many questions. Wait until we get inside."

The guard examined the ID card for a moment. Visions of them standing before a firing squad flashed through David's mind. Suddenly the guard handed back the card and signaled for them to enter. As they drove on, there was nothing in front of them but open space.

David remarked, "It looks like we're driving on an airfield."

"We are," she replied to his amazement.

Finally approaching a one-story building that seemed to stretch on for miles, she pulled up to the closest entrance and stopped the car. "Okay, let's go," she said.

David got out and followed her lead. She inserted the card into a slot and the door opened. As they entered, they saw groups of technicians intensely involved in their work. David remarked at the vastness of the structure.

Nancy said, "You haven't seen anything yet!"

She led him to an elevator. As they got in, David noticed that there were four levels. Nancy pushed number four, the lowest level.

Once again, he inquired, "Nancy, what is this place?"

As the elevator descended, she explained, "David, this was all, at one time, part of Tokyo Bay. It was part of a reclamation project started many yeas ago to build a new and expanded airport. Somewhere along the way, the JDS took it over and expanded it to this huge, modernized facility."

Before she could go any further, the elevator stopped and the doors opened. David moved cautiously as they emerged. He couldn't believe what he saw. He found himself repeating the same question over and over. "Nancy, what is this place?"

"Those were the exact words that I said to myself when I found this place," she whispered.

As they continued on, David exclaimed, "My God, Nancy, this place is a giant arsenal, an underground city built for what could only be the sole purpose of destruction." As he surveyed the area, his astonishment deepened and he said in utter disbelief, "My God, there's enough advanced, sophisticated weaponry down here to blow the entire world apart. Some of this stuff probably has never been seen by the outside world. They don't even know weapons like these have been invented."

However, the biggest shock was yet to come. Going a little farther, they came upon a sight that blew David's mind completely. He was standing at the entrance of an underground naval base, and as far as his eyes could see, there were submarines suspended by huge hoists over channels filled with water. "They look like enormous Jet Skis minus the propellers," David said to Nancy. "I'm guessing that they must be powered by magnetic hydro expulsion. Where do these channels lead?"

She replied, "Under Tokyo Bay."

David suddenly reeled at the stark reality. "My God, with a push of a button, this armada could be dropped into the channels and silently slither out into the ocean, creep up to our doorstep undetected, ring the bell, and blow us off the face of the earth." Turning to Nancy, he grabbed her hand tightly and said, "I've seen enough. Let's get the hell out of here."

"Not just yet," she replied. "This is not all that I brought you here to see."

David jokingly asked, "What the hell else can there be?"

She led him back to the elevator, this time stopping at the second floor. They exited, and David was horrified at the spectacle before him. "Nancy, tell me that this is just a bad dream. This just can't be reality."

There were at least a thousand incubators lined up in rows. Each row contained human embryos at different stages of growth, busily being attended to by a team of technicians. David looked at Nancy and said, "We should have brought a camera. No one will ever believe this … No one will ever believe this."

"David, this is the reason that Toysukibishi wants Tasco's intelligence gene. So you see your committee members were right. They certainly were not overreacting."

"Okay, I get the picture," David whispered furiously. "Now let's get the hell out of here!"

Nancy wasn't ready to leave. She quickly pulled David back to the elevator. She excitedly explained, "I have to try to exit on the last level. I have been hesitant to push the third floor selection." Nancy pushed the elevator button marked three. The computer on the elevator requested her identification card to be inserted. She did so, and the computer denied access to that floor. Nancy couldn't know that the computer also alerted Sam at the same time.

Sam saw that his daughter was in the high-security area. He spoke to her over the computer and advised her that he was on his way. "Don't leave the area," he advised. "You need my help to go any farther." Before he had finished speaking, four armed guards flanked the elevator door.

It seemed more like hours than minutes before her father appeared. He dismissed the guards and told his daughter, "Because of the genetic nature of your position here, you are entitled to see this area. You are and have been participating in this study. The button you pushed is beyond the scope of your position and is not available to you. I'm extremely proud of what we have accomplished here, and I will take you to the last level myself."

Sam led his daughter to the top-secret area of the JDS. They passed the intelligence testing area and through a full-length metal detector. The passageway to the next area was built of bulletproof glass and must have been at least one hundred feet long. At the end was a metal door that Sam had to use his thumbprint to enter.

David had been trying unsuccessfully to convince Tasco to release the intelligence gene. He had no way of knowing that Sam, with the help of his mole Shirley, had secured the gene years ago. This had been a well-kept secret until now.

The remarkable chamber ahead of them had the seating capacity for one thousand people at a time. This was the final educational facility for the armada that Sam had built. It was the place where the intelligent and growth specimens were groomed to make an invincible army. The general, in full-dress uniform, was addressing the room full of young cadets. "Each one of you is equivalent to a West Point graduate. You all have been trained to follow our master plan and execute it to the fullest. It is the wish of our president, who has just entered, that you succeed and bring this country back to its former glory."

The cadets all stood up and cheered. Sam was glowing with pride and Nancy hung back behind him, horrified at the sight before her.

Reason flooded her brain. She and David had to get out safely. This was not the time or the place to discuss semantics. Nancy praised her father and told him they had booked a gourmet restaurant for dinner. David's feeling of anxiety didn't subside until they were safely out of the JDS. Sam had told them the letters stood for Judgment Day Section. Deeply concerned for their safety after what they had just seen, David told Nancy, "Drop me off at the hotel. Then go home and pack a light bag. Meet me at the airport in the morning. I'm not going to leave Japan without you!"

She willingly agreed.

The following day, David and Nancy, along with Tasco's four-man committee a few steps behind, boarded a plane bound for the United

States. As David had instructed, Nancy only brought one bag, which she checked into regular baggage, and a black attaché case that she carried on with her.

Up to this point, there had been no conversation. The group seemed to be in deep thought, disturbed over what they had witnessed during the past few days, especially David. With what he had in his mind, he kept his mouth shut until they were safely airborne. Even then he chose his words carefully as he softly remarked to Nancy, "Wow, I don't ever remember being this nervous in my entire life. I thought someone was following me, beating a bass drum. However, I soon realized it was my own heart."

She giggled, mostly out of nervousness, and reached out to hold his hand.

"My God, Nancy! I feel like we're a couple of spies. What kind of a world are we living in? We work our butts off making great discoveries so humanity can take a step forward. Then along comes some demented geniuses, who distort our achievements and force the world to go backward again."

As they thought about it, the reality of the situation started sinking in. Throughout history many people had been killed for knowing much less than they did now. They couldn't help but feel fortunate that no one had caught them at the underground facility or interfered with their rapid departure from Tokyo.

As the security of being on an American plane heading for safety began to ease their tension, they settled back in their seats. With her arm wrapped around his, they both fell asleep.

When they landed in San Francisco, completing the first leg of their journey, everyone was asked to leave the plane for an hour. The plane had to be cleaned and refueled for their continuing flight to

New York. While they relaxed in the airport's lounge, David poured himself a beer that he had ordered. Nancy casually sipped her Pepsi from a straw as she leaned her elbows on the attaché case, keeping it snugly tucked on her lap.

David, unable to hold back his curiosity any longer, finally said, "You know, I watched you carry that thing onto the plane in Tokyo. You almost sat on it the entire trip, and now you're holding it securely on your lap." Jokingly he asked with a small laugh, "Is it filled with money?" She didn't reply. Pressing her further, he asked mysteriously, "Is it filled with jewels?"

"No, it's neither," she replied. Then she was silent again.

David, throwing in the towel, said, "Okay, sweetheart, I give up. What's in it?"

Knowing David would be shocked at her disclosure, Nancy hesitated momentarily to think about how to begin. Finally, in a low voice, she explained, "The other night, as we left the underground city, you told me to go straight home and pack a bag. Well, I didn't. I stopped of fat the labs first."

David exclaimed, "What the hell for?"

She opened the case, leaning it forward so he could see its contents. His eyes opened wide, and his face reflected the horror he felt.

"That's what for!" she said.

David, in a severe state of shock, managed a feeble reply. "Nancy, that's the Tamaki file, Toysukibishi's rapid-growth project. If they knew you had that, we never would have left Japan alive. I can't believe you took that kind of a risk."

"David, I had to. You can tell them all about the underground city, the sophisticated weaponry, and the naval base with those weird-looking submarines. They'll believe you because it's something that can be understood. However, this stuff"—she pointed to the Tamaki file—"no one would ever believe."

Displaying extreme caution, Nancy paused to lift the file slightly so she didn't have to remove it from the case. She revealed another file beneath it. "This is the real frightening one, David! It could be more devastating than that whole underground city. It contains a diabolical plan to infiltrate sperm banks around the world with Toysukibishi's genetically engineered genes, carrying Japanese traits. As these children grow into adulthood, taking on the characteristics of their maternal host, their brains will become genetically programmed to think pro-Japan. People all around the world won't know who their neighbors really are."

Nancy sadly continued, "David, if we don't stop Toysukibishi, the future will have a new generation of people born without freedom of thought, a race of brainwashed people."

David was stunned by what Nancy revealed to him. All he could say was "Hurry, close that thing and let's get back on that plane!"

CHAPTER 39

SAM PICKED UP THE phone and dialed his brother's hotline number. When Billy answered, Sam gave him a short briefing, telling him that Nancy had run off with David. He ordered Billy to do a background check on the Tasco four-man committee and a separate one on David Watson. "I want to know everything about him. Where was he born? Where did he go to school?"

Emphasizing the expected thoroughness of the report, he demanded, "Billy, I want to know how many times a day he goes to the bathroom! In addition, set up a meeting for this afternoon with our financial committee. If Tasco won't join us voluntarily, we'll buy the damn company!" As an afterthought, Sam said, "While you're at it, do a workup on all their major stockholders and have it ready for the meeting this afternoon." As he hung up the phone, Sam could feel his fingers tingling. The old panther's anxiety had peaked, preparing him for the inevitable attack.

Later that same day, Sam and his financial advisors formulated a plan for the acquisition of the entire Tasco Research Corporation, which in itself was not to be taken lightly. Throughout the years Tasco had become a giant conglomerate in its own right, and acquiring it would prove to be a formidable undertaking.

One week later, Billy walked into Sam's office and announced, "I have just secured the reports that you requested. In fact, we did a background workup for you on the rest of Tasco's board, as well." Hesitating for a moment, he placed a separate envelope on Sam's desk, saying, "This one will be of special interest to you. It contains all the information about David Watson."

As Sam read through David's background report, Billy could see his brother's expression of disbelief intensify. As he stared at the last page for what seemed an eternity, Sam finally regained his composure. He looked up at Billy and said, "Call for my pilot. Have him get the jet ready to leave for Seattle in one hour!"

The address Sam had given the taxi driver led them down a long, tree-lined private road, which was apparently the entrance to a large estate. The road eventually ended at a circular driveway surrounding a giant water fountain. Sam's heart began beating uncontrollably as his anxiety reached its crescendo. Upon exiting the taxi, he followed a heavily flowered path to a large, magnificent, white stone English Tudor.

After he apprehensively rang the bell, a servant answered the door. Sam announced himself, and she politely asked him to enter and wait there. He was overwhelmed by the enormity of the foyer and its huge crystal chandelier. As he momentarily stared at the splendid fixture, the servant returned and graciously requested, "Please follow me, Mr. Sagarra." Stopping in front of an exquisitely decorated living room, she motioned for him to proceed on his own.

As Sam entered the room, she was standing at the far end next to a small antique chair. She was thin and frail but stood erect. Her once long, fiery-red hair was now glistening sliver and cut short, just long enough to cover her earlobes. Her face, treated kindly by the years, was aglow with the pleasure of seeing him. As he approached her, Mickey began to smile, and he could see her beautiful green eyes still radiated their devilish gleam from within. They reached out and held each other's hands without speaking. As Sam held her, his mind flashed back through the years to the night she lit those red candles and to the exquisite feeling of making love to her.

After an hour of reminiscing, Mickey finally asked, "Sam, what are you really doing here in America?"

He told her about his consortium's interest in acquiring an American company and how, prior to any serious negotiations, they routinely secured a background check of all the owners and major stockholders. Sam stood up and walked a few feet away, slowly turning back to face Mickey. "Your name is on the report."

Mickey sat motionless and listened graciously as he continued. "You own a large portion of Tasco stock."

Mickey answered assertively, "Yes, I know of your desire to take over Tasco. Does that disturb you?"

Sam replied, "No, it doesn't. It's just that I haven't heard from you in all these years." As his voice raised slightly in a tone of anger, he said, "You just disappeared!"

Sam reached into his pocket and produced an envelope, holding it out for Mickey to take. "Then, almost fifty-five years later, you suddenly reappear in this." As she reached for the envelope, he said, "I'm just confused."

Mickey removed the contents of the envelope, and her hands began to tremble slightly as a small amount of perspiration built up on her forehead. Her mind started racing, flashing back to events from many years ago. Sam watched quietly and anxiously as Mickey read the report. When she was finished, she sat back and looked up at him. Sam looked into her eyes, those radiant green eyes that he had fallen in love with so many years ago.

Sitting down next to her, they both stared lovingly at each other. After a few minutes had gone by, trying futilely to keep from crying, Mickey finally broke the silence. With tears running down her cheeks, she said to Sam, "This report just about summarizes my whole life."

He couldn't contain his curiousity. "Mickey, this report is about David Watson. What does Margaret McGovern have to do with David Watson?"

Mickey, straining to put what had occurred into the proper words, said, "Sam, it was so long ago. It seems as though it was only a dream." She took a deep breath. "Sam, I had to get away. When my brother died in that crash, I blamed you a little. I couldn't get it out of my mind, no matter how I tried. I couldn't have loved you more, but I felt as though I was being pulled apart at the seams. My whole world was going crazy."

Sam just sat next to her and listened quietly as she searched for the right words to continue.

"While Japan was threatening war and anti-Japanese sentiment was raging, I was in love with a Japanese American guy, whose baby was growing inside me."

Sam pulled back in shocked amazement. "I don't understand! You were pregnant and you chose not to tell me? Why, Mickey, why?"

She replied softly, "I was afraid and confused. When I told my mother, she was horrified, and you have to believe me, Sam, neither she nor my father were racists. She knew how close the three of us were. You spent more time with Tommy and me than you did with your own family. You were like another son to her. After Tommy died, the picture of the two of you posing with that crazy car ..." Mickey stopped for a second trying to think of its name. ". . . Blazer! That's it! The Blazer."

Sam added, "Number one."

"That picture became my parents' shrine. My mother hung it on the living room wall and she'd sit and look at it for hours. She loved you," Mickey lamented. "She loved the three of us, even though we drove her nuts. However, she insisted that if I was going to have your baby, it would never work because of all the insanity going on in the world at the time. She convinced me to have an abortion. I was to go and stay with my aunt and uncle in Arizona. When it was over and I had recuperated, I would remain with them and go to college.

"I had been there for a few weeks, waiting for the arrangements to be made, when I realized that I couldn't go through with it. When I called Mother and told her of my decision to have our baby, she tried to talk me out of it. When she finally realized that she couldn't, she tried to convince me to come home, but I refused."

Sam asked, "Mickey, why wouldn't you go home?"

Mickey replied, "I thought that if I came home, somehow she'd convince me to have the abort ion. I just wasn't going to give up the baby."

Sam asked, "Why didn't you get in touch with me?"

Mickey answered simply and honestly, "I don't know. I guess I was afraid and confused. I needed time to sort things out. The only thing that I was sure of was that I wasn't going to give up my baby! However, by the time I did try to reach you, I was already seven months pregnant and you were gone. Your whole family was gone. The only one left was Sarah, and she was in a sanatorium, convalescing from the trauma of that brutal rape.

"After I gave birth … oh, it was a boy and I named him Mark," Mickey added, almost as an afterthought, "I called Mother immediately asking her to try to find you. She told me that shortly after the bombing of Pearl Harbor, she had tried to reach you to inform you that your parents had not returned from California. Not knowing where you were, she had Father contact the naval department, which traced you to Hawaii.

"Mother's letter was returned because of some kind of communication blackout. After a few months, she tried again, only to get the same results. The large number of casualties, due to the Pearl Harbor attack, was finally being made public. She assumed that you were dead and that for some reason, maybe because you were Japanese, the war department was holding back the information.

"Sam, I was so frightened and terrified of being alone, but I couldn't go back to Chicago. There were too many memories there, mostly good, but I needed something different. I didn't know exactly what that would be; I just knew it wasn't back there.

"When Mark was a little more than a year old, I left him with my aunt and uncle. Without any particular destination in mind, I started out to make a new life for the two of us. There was a newly formed biological research company that I had recently read about." Looking at Sam, Mickey reminded him, "You remember my interest in biology?" He nodded and she continued. "Well, I sent them a letter describing my enthusiasm over their work, and they responded by offering me a job. It was nothing more than maintaining their progression charts, but it was a job and far enough away. So I was off to Seattle."

CHAPTER 40

"Karl Watson and his brother, Dan, were the founders of Tasco. There were only four employees at that time, three research scientists and me. My job was to track and control all the testing, and I loved the work. Karl and Dan had some amazing theories that would open up many new frontiers. All they needed was sufficient funding. That's where I was able to help." Glancing at Sam, Mickey continued her story. "You remember my father, 'Fast Jack,' always ready for a good game of craps. Only this time he was unable to use his bank's funding because of some law prohibiting the crossing of state lines. He invested his own money, everything he had! Tasco's theories and tests helped bring about some of our greatest medical breakthroughs, developing life-saving drugs that had previously been only figments of the imagination. The company went public in the early fifties, and the rest is history.

"I had only been there for two months when Karl started taking me to all the local social functions, introducing me as one of his best discoveries. Six months later he asked me to marry him. At first I declined, telling him he didn't know enough about me, although he already knew about Mark and the two of them got along splendidly, forming a special bond in a very short time.

"Both of Karl's parents had recently died in an automobile accident. All he had left was his brother. I think we all just needed each other. Karl also loved baseball, and when the season opened, he took Mark to his first game. He brought him home fully outfitted, with his own bat, ball, and glove, and topped it off with a cap. When football season opened, they started all over again. Mark loved him! Anyway, Karl persisted and we were married."

Sam asked, "Did you love him?"

Mickey hesitated for a moment, pondering the question and finally replied, "I believe I did." She started thinking back and corrected herself. "Yes, I did. He was a wonderful, unselfish man, and we had a good life together."

Sam asked, "Did you have any children with him?"

Mickey replied, "Yes, a daughter, Marcy, presently living in New York. She works for a subsidiary of Tasco, leading its research department. Like her father, her head is full of theories and ideas to help mankind. In fact, it's her group that has made those recent genetic breakthroughs, splicing genes, transplanting genes, engineering new genes. I don't know. It's all too confusing for me. I must be getting old." A little smile appeared on her lovely face.

Sam kept questioning her. "How about Mark?"

Mickey paused and took a deep breath. "Mark graduated from college and became a research chemist for Tasco. During his second year in college, he came home on Christmas Eve to exchange gifts. Karl and I got him a new gold watch that he had once admired. His gift to us was a little more unique. He brought us a daughter-in-law, Helen.

"Helen was a sweet girl he had met at college. They had so much in common that falling in love was so natural. We were completely taken by surprise. He hadn't told us about his plan to marry Helen before coming home. We didn't know anything about her, and he thought that I would object, so he was completely surprised by my joyous and overwhelming approval. They were a beautiful couple. Sam, they reminded me so much of us. I wanted to help them in any way I could, but they didn't need anything but each other. They were extremely happy.

"After Mark joined the company, they bought a little house in the valley. Shortly after moving in, his reserve unit was called to active duty and sent to Korea. He was killed in action a few months later, never knowing he had a son, a son named David."

Mickey looked at Sam, hesitating for a second with a patient smile on her face, while Sam concentrated on her face. He appeared to be in a state of hypnosis, not knowing what other surprises she had in store for him. Mickey finally broke the silence. "So you see, we really did do something together after al l, Sam. David is our grandson."

"My God, Mickey, this is like a soap opera. David met my daughter, Nancy, in Japan. They have fall en in love, and she has returned to New York with him, where they plan to get married as soon as possible." Sam humorously added, "By a peculiar twist of fate, David happens to be marrying his aunt."

The reality of the situation seemed to become even more confusing as Sam lamented to Mickey, "In my early years, you and Tommy were the only bright spots in my life. When he was killed and you left, I was devastated. After the war, feeling there was nothing left for me in America, I returned with my parents to Japan. I built an empire there and used its power to wage a vendetta against the racist bigots who caused Tommy's death and destroyed the honor of my family. The only happiness I have known is my marriage to Christine and my daughter, Nancy.

"Now you inform me that we had a son who was killed in Korea, and his son, my grandson, wants to marry my daughter. I came here to solve a mystery, and I'm afraid that for the first time in my life, I don't know what to do."

Mickey replied assertively, as she always did. "Sam, there isn't anything we can do." Reaching into her pocket, she produced a telegram and held it out for him to see. She told him what it said. "They were married this morning! "They're going on with their lives, and I'm sure they will be happy." Laughing, she added, "Besides, look at all the fun they will have trying to solve the riddle of the Sagarras, Watsons, and McGoverns."

Sam managed a chuckle as he leaned over to kiss her on the cheek. "Mickey, you always were full of surprises. I just wish that you hadn't waited so long to spring this one. I have never stopped thinking about you. You have always been in my heart."

Tears ran down her cheeks as Sam's mind flashed back to the first time he had kissed her. He remembered how she had sneaked up from behind to scare him and caused him to touch the loose distributor wire, sending a jolt through both of their bodies. When he turned around, she had been stunned, and her beautiful fiery-green eyes were tearing profusely. He could still remember her sweet aroma when they embraced as though it had only happened yesterday. He brought himself back to reality, and with tears in their eyes, they wished each other well and said good-bye.

CHAPTER 41

When Sam arrived at the airport, his private plane was waiting, engines revving, and ready to depart. Upon entering, his voice reflected a tone of urgency as he instructed the pilot, "Get me back to Tokyo as quickly as possible!"

Flying above the clouds halfway across the Pacific Ocean, his body was overtaken by a deep anxiety as he thought of the irony of the situation. First, as an American, he took part in the destruction of Japan. Now he was helping Japan set in motion the destruction of America and possibly the entire world.

Reason had finally set in. He had to get back to Tokyo and try to reverse this catastrophic dilemma. His mind reflected on the seventy years of his life as a dozen thoughts entered it simultaneously. He thought of his first love, Mickey; of the cross-country race that he and Tommy won; and of Tommy's brutal, untimely death. Memories surfaced of his brother Char lie with his fifty-mile-radius, girl-finding ability, and of Sarah and Stan together in the sanitorium. The horror of the years that his parents spent in the concentration camp flashed through his mind, his love for Christine and Nancy, and finally all the wasted years he had spent consumed with revenge. An overwhelming feel ing of panic set in as he realized that he was running out of time.

Suddenly, as the clouds parted, he could see the ocean below. It was covered with little specks as far as the eye could see. He blinked to clear his eyes as he stared in shocked disbelief. The actuality of what he was seeing stunned him. Those tiny specks were ships, his armada of Japanese warships, and they were heading toward the United States. He could see the command ship below, and he knew the admiral who would be leading the attack. Sam could visualize him looking through his binoculars at the vast open sea, checking to make sure that everything was clear ahead. Realizing that he was already too late, he pathetically exclaimed, "Oh, my God! What have I done!"

The copilot came running back as he heard his boss scream, "Please forgive me!"

ABOUT THE AUTHOR

Discrimination is an ugly word. It's not something that you're born with; it's something that's taught. Most immigrants in the United States have faced some sort of discrimination, and many books have been written about the subject. My book relates to the tribulations of a Japanese family for the better part of the twentieth century.

As a young Jewish girl, born in Brooklyn, New York, I got my first job through a headhunter. I was just sixteen years old when I went to work on Wall Street for a banking investment firm. The employees were from all over the New York City area. The experience was invaluable. It taught me how to work and get along with and enjoy all types of people.

My husband and I live in South Carolina. When we decided to retire, we picked a state that had a change of seasons. My philosophy is be active and enjoy.